A FRANK DALTON THRILLER

DEADLY TIDES

JONATHAN SHIPPERLEY

CONTENTS

Willow, Aidan, Gavin and Anna.

Love you guys. Always.

"There is only one plot — things are not as they seem."

—Jim Thompson

PROLOGUE

Long rolling waves, tattered and disorganized when they hit the shore, fizzled out in the sands of North Padre Island. An evening sea breeze blowing from offshore brought a subtle freshness that barely overcame the pungent odor of excavator-piled mounds of seaweed, a common sight during sargassum season on the Texas coast.

A few miles further south of the residential section of North Padre Island and deep into the undeveloped section of the coastline, four men appeared out of the surf, heads swiveling, shedding their masks and fins. A coyote lifted its head, watching from the dunes, alerted by the movement. Sniffing intensely, waiting to see if these new creatures were predators or prey, fight, or flight ready to kick in.

The four men sped up as they hit the beach and ran in a crouch toward the cover of the dunes, some thirty feet from the shoreline. The coyote stood its ground for a moment, but sensing these men were more than it could handle, silently slunk off to find something more tangible to eat.

This beach was the northernmost part of an approximately sixty-six-mile barrier island stretching all the way to the Rio Grande, the erstwhile border with Mexico. It was once one island, but a manmade channel in the 1950s split Padre Island National Seashore into the north and south, though most of it is still a national park, untouched by man.

The four men were aided in their stealth beach landing by the gloomy night, the moon brooding behind interlaced finger fluffs of white. The night air also brought the faint chug-chug-chug of a single-screw diesel engine. The vessel, a shrimp catcher hailing from Mexico, slowly and calmly made way, furthering its distance from the shoreline as the sound gradually faded. When it was far enough offshore, it turned due south, back toward Mexico.

Each man carried a black drybag on his back, and kneeling in the sand, each of them operated as one. There was no need for words, unnecessary at this point as they had trained extensively for this mission, and each man knew what to do. They removed their bags from their backs and emptied the contents, several sealed plastic bags tumbling from each backpack to the sand. Inside the plastic bags, tightly wound muslin protected the contents, a Kel-Tec SUB-2000 9mm folding carbine. This second-generation weapon had a multi-mag grip, allowing the user to swap out magazines from several manufacturers. It folded in half and weighed about four and a quarter pounds, which was perfect for carrying in a backpack.

The infiltration plan the four men followed to gain access to the United States unobserved was straightforward in design and execution. The routes were already used by the cartels for drug dumps, so logistically, it wasn't that much harder to carry four men into America instead of drugs. Essentially, the plan relied on only two things: intelligence gathering and simplicity.

A few days earlier, a small and rusty but serviceable shrimper, hailing from the Mexican seaport of Tampico, in the southeastern part of the state of Tamaulipas, some five hundred miles south of Corpus Christi, Texas, headed offshore with a crew of three.

And four passengers.

The vessel steamed out to sea far enough that the crew knew they could circumnavigate detection by the U.S. Coast Guard, then turned toward their target zone just south of Corpus Christi, Texas. The vessel's modus operandi called for large bales of drugs—normally cocaine—to be dumped into the Gulf of Mexico. Waterproof and packed tightly together the drugs would drift onto shore where they would be collected by cartel members in four-wheel-drive vehicles. On this trip, however, there were no drugs, only people, and these people could swim, so the vessel's captain did not have to worry as much about tides and set and drift and didn't need to approach the shoreline as closely.

Avoidance of the authorities was not left to dumb luck, though. That was where the intelligence gathering came in. With millions of dollars in street value at stake, they left nothing to chance. The cartels relied on information for smooth operations, and they gathered it through bribes, extortion, threats, and the sheer hubris of humanity. The magnitude of their intelligence gathering was epic, made simpler by loose lips on Facebook, Instagram, Snapchat, and other social media.

The men, now hidden in the sand dunes, shed their wetsuits, burying them in the sand. Underneath, they were dressed in board shorts and tank tops—regular beach attire. The colors looked muted, and the clothes appeared worn, all designed to allow the men to blend. They kept their Kel-Tec carbines in their backpacks, within easy reach should they need them, but this particular illegal port of entry to the United States was designed for its lack of patrols. A towel thrown over their shoulders completed the disguises. Just four guys out to have some fun on the beach. When daylight broke, they hoped to look like wandering tourists should anyone see them.

They walked for several miles along the beach, keeping a quick and steady pace, hard in the sand, but they had trained for this. They kept an eye ahead and behind, not expecting trouble, but they hadn't come this far to be sloppy. The saltwater of the Gulf had dried on their skin, thin rivulets of sweat making tracks down their faces. It was hot even at night in South Texas.

After two hours of quiet walking, the surf and scuff of feet on sand the only sounds, a dull glow gradually appeared on the horizon, lights shimmering in the distance, and they knew they were approaching Bob Hall Pier at Padre Bali Park. This meant they were about to enter the populated area of North Padre Island, and this was the most likely place someone would see them. Time for the four men to be hypervigilant.

The men did not know each other's names. They were only known to each other as Alpha, Bravo, Charlie, and Delta. The men were perfect for the mission as they had no distinguishing features, looked like any other American citizen, and spoke excellent English. This was, of course, because they were American citizens, born and raised, and it was ironic, considering the mission they were on, proud of their country. But this was why they were here. Because they *were* proud. They knew without a doubt that the government had to be stopped. It had to be torn down. It had to be made aware that America had its own problems that needed fixing, not to be the police of the world. America first, last and always. Fix your own problems first. They were going to ensure the U.S. did just that.

Alpha held up his arm, bent at the elbow, his hand in a fist, signaling to stop. Scarcely discernible in the distance, a single set of headlights crawled down the beach. The men scrambled up the dunes and lay prone out of sight, hoping this was just some teenagers driving far enough from the lights of the pier for some privacy. But better to be ready than to blow the mission. Although they were dressed in beach clothes, it was dark and would still look peculiar to have four dudes walking the beach this far south, so they hid.

The vehicle lights drew closer, and the engine roar became noticeable over the surf. As it got closer, the emergency lights mounted on the roof, although not energized, were silhouetted in the night sky, identifying the vehicle as some sort of law enforcement.

The vehicle stopped almost perpendicular to the four men, and both front doors opened.

"I told you this was garbage duty," Special Agent Joe Miner said.

"Relax, will you?" Special Agent Glen Browning replied. "What's with you tonight, anyway? It's gorgeous out here. The waves, the beach. You could be stuck inside manning a radio or something."

"Sure could. And in the corner, the TV would be on, tuned into the game. Or I could have been sitting at a bar watching the game. You do know the World Series was tonight, right? The Astros. Ringing any bells? I could be supping on a nice cold one, but no, Glen says we need to patrol. Glen says—"

"Glen says he's had enough of your whiny bullshit for one night, Joe. Knock it off. We're out here because we get paid to do this. You know we had intel that there would be a drug drop tonight."

"And we've what? Patrolled this area like six times already tonight and every night for a week. Admit it, the intel was crap." Miner waved his arms around. "You see any mysterious bales of weed, unmarked packages of hashish? No, the biggest horde of dope out here is us two dildos. What were we gonna do anyway, drive right up on them? They can probably see our headlights for miles."

"That's not the point, and you know it. Waving the flag is usually deterrent enough. You know how it works. They drop the shit off by boat, it floats in, and then some other guys come and collect it. They're not going to take it out on a pack mule. They need a vehicle, too. We'd easily spot them or the drugs."

"You hope. Damn," Miner said, waving his phone around at the night sky. "There's no cell service out here. How am I supposed to check the score? I can't even see who won."

"You can watch the highlights when we get back." Browning kicked the sand around for a second. "Come on, get back in the truck. We'll go another mile or two and then call it a night. You can see who won your precious game."

"Good. I'm gonna smoke first, though, and I need to pee." Miner scuffed over to the dunes and unzipped. Letting out a sigh as he felt the release. He made schoolboy circles in the sand with the stream of urine, the waft of steam drifting upward. Finished, he zipped up, pulled out his cigarettes, and lit one, the flare of the lighter momentarily lighting up a small area of the dunes, walked a few feet, and sat down on a large driftwood log facing the water.

"Joe. Why don't you come back over here?" Browning said.

"Yeah, yeah, I'm coming. What's the rush? Can't see shit right now. The lighter fucked with my night vision."

"I know. Hey, why don't you walk back over here anyway? I need you to look at something. It looks like the tire may be going flat. Maybe we ran over something."

"Seriously? Damn it. It's probably a nail from all those idiots that use pallets for firewood. Now, I'll miss the whole game." Miner got up and shuffled in the sand over to where Browning was standing, the vehicle now between them and the dunes.

"Dude, which tire? This one looks fine. Are you sure—"

"Yeah, right? Looks a bit low. Maybe we should go back to base," Browning said loudly, and then quieter, "Back there when you lit your cigarette." Miner didn't say anything but nodded, realizing this wasn't about the tire. "I thought I saw a face in the dunes. Hard to tell the distance, but it can't be more than a few yards from where you were standing. I can't be sure of what I saw, but if it is someone, they're not hiding for anything good." Miner made a move to look, but Browning grabbed him. "Don't look. Listen, this is what we're going to do. We're going to get back in the vehicle, drive down a ways, and turn around. We'll put the brights and spotlight on and turn into him, her or them. The lights will fuck with their night vision, and maybe we can roust them out. Look, it's probably just kids smoking pot, nothing to worry about, but maybe it's what we're out here for."

"Want to call it in?"

"I thought about it. Who's on comms watch tonight?"

"Ricky, I think."

"That settles it then. I'm not calling that prick just so he can make fun of us when we find it's a log or something. We can always radio in later."

Miner hesitated but then nodded. "Agreed."

"Let's get back in the truck, buddy," Browning said overly loud. "Head back home. Nothing to see here."

Miner and Browning slid back into the front seats of the truck. Browning, behind the wheel, started it up and drove down the beach for about two hundred yards, then executed a lazy three-point turn and drove back slowly to where they'd stopped before, keeping as close to the water as he could. Right before they got to the point where Browning thought he saw the face in the dunes, he energized the strobe and spotlights, lighting up the night sky, and turned the vehicle to face the dunes so it was head-on and mashed the accelerator, forcing the vehicle through the sand toward the dunes.

Immediately, the rat-a-tat of automatic fire from multiple weapons hit the vehicle, shattering the windshield and dousing the lights, save for one lonely blue strobe. Miner and Browning both ducked below the dash for cover, Browning hitting the brakes, the nose of the SUV diving lower in the sand.

"Shit," Miner said. "Motherfuckers have machine guns. So much for kids smoking pot. Want to call it in now, genius?"

Browning, still ducked below the dash, dragged the transmission into reverse and punched the accelerator, trying to widen the gap between whoever was in the dunes and their vehicle. The vehicle lurched and then bogged down in the thick, heavy sand, wheels spinning.

"Four-wheel drive, put it in four-wheel drive," Miner yelled over the steady staccato beat of weapons fire.

"Call for backup, Joe," Browning said, engaging four-wheel drive and goosing the engine. The SUV surged backward and then suddenly sagged, bogged down in the sand as the tires were shot out.

Miner reached above his head for the dash-mounted mic, mashed the transmit button, and yelled, "Shots fired, shots fired, taking automatic fire, time now, unknown number of hostiles, say again shots fired, shots fired, request immediate backup. Location, national seashore, approximately one mile south of Padre Bali Park. Request immediate backup, over." Miner let go of the transmit button and waited a second for an answer. When he didn't receive one, he repeated the same message and glanced at the radio. "Shit," he said, "the radio took a bullet. It's dead. Do you have cell service?"

Browning, having no luck with the vehicle now that the tires had been blown out, had his Glock 19 pistol out and pointed through the shattered windshield. He rapidly fired three shots into the dunes, deafening in the confined space of the SUV.

Browning pulled out his phone and glanced at it. "No service. The truck's OOC. We need to get to the trunk and get the long guns out. We don't stand a chance with pistols against whatever they're using."

Miner had his Glock 19 out now and fired two shots.

"What's the plan?" Miner said.

"Don't get shot."

"Anything else?"

"We make the best of it. Listen, when I say, we'll open the front doors and climb into the back seat, then open those doors. I'll lay down some cover fire for you and vice versa. Then we can get out the back doors and behind the vehicle. Ready?"

A single nod, eyes wide.

"On three. One, two, three."

Pop, pop, pop. The sound of Miner's Glock was loud in the confined space of the vehicle but quiet compared to the staccato bursts of the automatic fire. Browning jammed open his door and crawled into the back seat, opening the back door. Miner crawled back as Browning opened fire, following the same process.

"Now." Browning and Miner flung themselves to the sand, and army crawled to the back of the vehicle. Opening the trunk gave them access to the lockbox of M4 carbines and Remington M870 pump-action shotguns. The open doors of the vehicle gave them a little more cover.

They each grabbed an M4, slammed a fresh 30-round magazine home, and pulled back the bolt handle, readying the weapon to fire. "Let's light these fuckers up," Browning said, taking the left side of the vehicle. Miner took the right, and together they shot at the dunes in short, controlled bursts of three rounds. The noise was even more deafening than the pistol shots, the acrid smell of gunpowder almost overwhelming. In a few seconds, the magazines ran dry, and Browning and Miner ducked behind the vehicle again to reload. "I think we got them, Joe. They've stopped shooting."

"What? I can't hear you," Miner said. "The gunfire, you know?"

"I said, I think we've got them, "Browning said, mouthing the words clearly.

Miner nodded, understanding now. "Yeah," he said. "Those fuckers don't know what hit them. Take that, you motherfuckers. Teach you to shit on the Coast—"

"No. Keep down," Browning said as Miner stood up.

A single shot rang out from the dunes, hitting Miner, separating his jaw from his head, blood spraying in an arc behind him.

"No," Browning whispered in shock. "No, you stupid motherfucker. No."

Browning crawled to Miner and dragged him behind the vehicle, but it was too late. He didn't even need to check for a pulse. Rage crept through Browning. The adrenaline, the gunfight, the death of his partner, all made the world narrow to a pinpoint. Forgetting his training, he scooped up Miner's weapon in his left hand, his own in his right, and ran toward the dunes, firing each gun from the hip like a film star in the last action scene from a movie.

Browning let out a raw battle cry, fueling his blind rage, pressing him onward. Guns still blazing, heart pumping, legs pushing him faster forward on the sand. Almost there. He could see them hiding in the shadows. First the left, then the right gun clicked on empty. Browning kept pressing the trigger, then threw the guns away in disgust, but he kept going.

One of the four men shot back, narrowly missing Browning, hitting the sand beside him.

"That the best you've got?" he shouted, continuing his mad dash up the beach. Another shot, this one to his right. The third caught him in the gut, and Browning collapsed to the sand onto his knees, his hands pressing his stomach.

Alpha stood and walked unhurriedly down to Browning, scanning the beach left and right. Alpha didn't say anything. He looked at Browning and shot him once in the head, between his eyes.

The ensuing silence was almost as deafening as the gunfire had been. Of the four men in the dunes, two were dead. Alpha, seeing red and blue flashing lights coming down the beach, clambered back up the dunes, nodded to the remaining man, and they hastily gathered the others' weapons and packs and took off, leaving their fallen behind. The mission was too critical to compromise. It would be that much harder now with only half a team.

The two surviving terrorists ran across the dunes, looking for the National Seashore access road that would take them into North Padre Island and then into

Corpus Christi, San Antonio and Houston. They could not be caught, would not be caught.

ONE

The tinny-sounding speakers in my voice-activated headphones sprang to life as the pilot said, "Brace yourselves, brace yourselves, we're coming in hard."

The rotors of the helo started winding down, the turbine above my head making a screeching, grinding racket that could still be heard above the warning klaxon. Flashing strobe lights illuminated the cabin.

"Prepare for a water landing. Assume the crash position." The pilot's voice sounded strained.

The five-point harness held me securely against the seat back, so I couldn't move much. I put my hands behind my head, elbows forward, and did the best I could.

The impact and shock of the landing were nothing compared to the fear flooding through me as the cabin rapidly filled with water, bursting through the windows and around the door's seams. I grappled with a pocket on my PFD and shook out the re-breather that would give me approximately three minutes of air as the water rapidly filled the cabin. The aircraft lurched as it tipped sideways, then turned turtle and slipped below the surface and sank to the bottom. My heart beat a million miles an hour, my stomach lurched, and I inwardly cursed this shitty contraption I was trapped in.

It was almost pitch black, and I was now upside down, underwater. I shoved the re-breather in my mouth, activating it when I inhaled. I was now on a timer and only had three minutes to breathe before I ran out of air. The cabin lurched again as it settled on the bottom, and I fought with the buckles of my seat restraint. I had a momentary spasm as I wondered if my air supply was full, but I could do nothing about it now. I finally got free of the restraint after what felt like five minutes, but knew it could only be a few seconds, and felt around for the exit. I was disoriented. Nothing felt right. I could feel myself breathing quicker, panicking. I had to clamp down on my emotions. I'd only run out of air faster if I panicked.

I felt something kick me in the shoulder, slowing my momentum, probably one of the crew, but I couldn't see shit and pressed onward. I had to go about six feet forward and turn right and out. Or was it left? We were upside down. Shit. Fuck. I couldn't have much air left. I could feel my heart racing faster, the adrenaline kicking in, spurring me headfirst into what I prayed wasn't oblivion. I would not give in. I would not succumb. I found the exit almost by accident and kicked free of the helicopter. My air ran out as I started my ascent, and I almost gagged as I spat it out, useless to me now. I pulled the tag on my PFD, and the sudden surge of compressed CO_2 filled the inflation bags and pushed me up.

I could see a glimmer of light above me, and then my head surfaced, and I drew in a lungful of joyous, fresh, chlorinated air.

I swam to the side of the pool, rested for a moment, breathing hard, and pulled myself out, sitting on the side, legs still in the water. The lights came on, and I could see the empty cage at the bottom of the pool. Underwater flight simulator, they called it. Dunker training. A twisted experiment, I called it.

"Thought you wouldn't make it for a moment, Dalton. We were about to send the diver in to get you," said a voice from behind me. One of the rescue swimmers, no doubt.

"Fuck this shit," I muttered under my breath, heaving myself to my feet, still breathing hard. "Tell me again why we need to do this?"

"Because, Special Agent Dalton," Smith said, coming over from the bleachers, "if you are ever in a real helo crash," he pronounced it he-low, "in water, you'll know how to survive and get free."

Tobias Smith, the acting special agent in charge, and my boss walked up to me. "And besides, it's fantastic entertainment. Where else can I watch the great Frank Dalton stress out?" He threw a towel at me, which I grabbed and rubbed my face with, shaking the water from my ears.

"I don't like being strapped in, turned upside down, and dropped into a fucking pool. Do we crash helos onto the tarmac to see if we survive that?"

"Oh, come on. It wasn't that bad."

"It was. Gets worse every year." I shook my head from side to side to remove the remaining water from my ears. "I enjoy being on the water, not so much in it."

"Come on, get dried off and dressed." Smith's smile faltered. "We have work to do."

I sensed his change in tone. "What's going on?"

He looked around and lowered his voice. "Not here. Meet me outside in the G-ride, and I'll fill you in. Make it quick. This is as important as it gets."

With those ominous words hanging over me, I didn't take long to dry off and change. I slipped my badge on over my belt, cinched my Glock 19 pistol to my side, and walked outside.

Smith's car was easy to spot, as most G-rides are. I opened the passenger door of the sedan and poked my head in.

"You're not planning to drive me anywhere in this, right?" I asked.

After a rocky start a few months ago, Smith and I cemented our professional relationship. I didn't trust him initially because I thought he was involved with Timmy "Batman" Black, an underhanded villain who had kidnaped my partner, Jessica Carter. The investigation revealed it wasn't Smith though who was crooked, but his boss, Special Agent in Charge Lewis. The big boss. He'd been taking bribes from Black for years and feeding him intel on our operations. We eventually caught Black, which didn't end well for him and rescued Carter, but

Lewis was still in the wind. But that's a story for another day, and I hoped those dangerous currents had calmed. Suffice to say, we'd cleared the air. Smith was the acting SAC until they found a suitable replacement or made his position permanent. I was keeping my fingers crossed for permanent.

"I am," Smith said. "Get in. We have to drive to North Padre Island."

"Not in that we don't. Let's get my truck. I have all my gear in it, and you know I don't do sedans anymore. Not after last year." The last time I'd driven government-issued sedans, they'd been shot at and blown up. I needed something a little heftier after that experience.

To his credit, Smith didn't argue; he just got out, and we walked over to my rig, which was still a G-ride but permanently assigned to me. It was a Ford F-150 with heavily tinted windows, a special lockbox in the bed that held all my toys and gadgets, and a few extra bells and whistles I'd installed myself. Don't tell GSA.

"North Padre, you said?" I put the truck in drive and started moving in that direction.

"Yeah. Take the Padre Bali Park exit to the beach. I'll fill you in on what happened. Carter is already on scene."

Smith told me about the shootout the night before. The first responders had determined there was nothing they could do for Miner or Browning. They'd also discovered two other deceased individuals in the dunes. The CSI techs and the medical examiner were on scene.

"You should have called me, Tobias. I didn't need to do the dunker training this morning. This is way more important."

"Yes, it is way more important, but you were months overdue for training. If you didn't get it in, I'd have to bench you. I wasn't going to have you skip out again and then have you grounded during the investigation. I made a command decision and that was it. Okay?"

I grumbled a reply, knowing he was right and continued driving to the beach exit. I was familiar with where we were going, having driven down the beach on multiple occasions. The beach was hard-packed sand, a regular sedan could drive on it, but then further on the sand became softer, and you really needed a four-wheel drive. The area was great for families, friends, and kids. The Gulf of Mexico this time of the year was usually bathwater warm, and super shallow. You could park anywhere, reverse up to the sea, open your trunk, and voila, no humping chairs, coolers or umbrellas. Bonfires were allowed too, and many a night I'd sat with a few buddies, sipping a brew, listening to the surf smash onto the beach and watching the crackling embers of a fire. The night stars were also fantastic, with no streetlights for miles to interfere. If you had a telescope, it was out of this world.

However, this trip wasn't for pleasure. No beer, no fires, no jokes.

About half a mile along the beach, we spotted the flashing lights of emergency vehicles and knew we had the right spot. I pulled up on the outskirts of the media tape—tape that had been explicitly erected to keep looky-loos and the media out. I flashed my badge at the cop on guard duty, and he let us through, moving a makeshift entrance made from a couple of cones, and we drove another hundred yards to the scene.

Huge tents had been set up in the dunes around the two dead CGIS agents and their SUV. Screens had been placed around the tents, partly so the CSI teams could work in the shade and partly to preserve any evidence. The tents also helped to keep prying eyes away, especially the media.

I parked, and we got out, heading for the command tent. It was actually just a couple of tables and some laptops, a small Honda generator running quietly in the corner.

I smiled as I saw Special Agent Jessica Carter, my heart skipping half a beat. Even after months of being together, every time I saw her, I just had to smile. I was a lucky man. I knew this was a shitty situation but tell that to my heart.

"Hey, Jess," I said.

She turned, and her smile lit up her face. "Frank," she said, "Missed you this morning."

"Yeah, I had to leave early so they could try and drown me in the pool."

"Dunker training again?"

"You know it," I said, grimacing and shivering at the same time.

Carter had been a rookie agent six months ago, new to the job and assigned with me to investigate Black. After a rocky start, we'd become fast friends and then something more, something better. It all went to shit when she went to grab a bite to eat at lunchtime and Black had her kidnaped by one of his henchmen. We were getting too close to an arrest, so this was his attempt to stop the investigation and stop me.

He went too far.

She was tortured.

Brutally.

With the help of some high-level operatives, we'd found that bastard Black and launched a raid on his island fortress in the Caribbean.

The stress of what Black did to her took its toll physically and mentally. When I found her on the island, she was in shock and very confused about what had happened. The docs had said that with time she would be fine but would need significant counseling. I didn't know and still wasn't sure if they understood what she'd been through. What I knew was that I loved her, and while the physical scars were gone, the emotional ones were still underneath, causing her some understandable stress and crippling flashbacks from time to time.

"Oh, he did fine," Smith said. "He loves dunker training, don't you Frank?" Smith punched me lightly on the shoulder. I glared at him for a moment but then gave up and offered him a faint smile.

"So, what have we got?" I said, changing the subject.

"Put these on first, and I'll show you," Carter said. We both put on Tyvek suits, rubber booties, and blue nitrile gloves, matching her outfit. Standard procedure, so we didn't screw up the crime scene. No use adding our personal DNA debris and giving the CSI guys more work to do. It must be hard enough with all this sand anyway.

Dressed out, we followed Carter from the command tent over to another, where the shot-up SUV was. The vehicle was a wreck and looked sad, sunk down to its rims. Every window, including the windshield, was shattered. Multiple bullet holes riddled the front, doors, and top. All four tires were shredded, and the insides looked all ripped to hell. What a fucking mess. Just behind the car, a sheet covered what could only have been a body. I'd seen my fair share of dead people, maybe even helped one or two along on their journey to the other side, but it was different when it was one of your own. The firepower aimed at the vehicle was astonishing. I couldn't even comprehend what it must have been like.

The medical examiner, Doctor Kelly Hutchins, was poking around inside the vehicle, similarly dressed like us. She was the chief medical examiner for the Coast Guard Investigative Service and worked with us on all our cases. We were old friends.

"Stop where you are," she said, getting out of the SUV and catching sight of us. "I'll come over to you." She carefully extricated herself and walked over. "Frank, Tobias, wish I could say it was good to see you, but under these circumstances…"

I nodded to her. "Can you give us a rundown, doc?"

"I can. As you probably know, two agents died last night. I can put the time of death at about zero three, maybe three thirty. Miner is back here under the cloth. Browning is about halfway between here and the dunes. They're both deceased, both from high velocity rounds. I'll let you know in more detail after I've completed the autopsy in what caliber you're looking for. Death appears to have been instantaneous for Miner who had one shot to the head. Browning had multiple gunshot wounds, but it still would have been quick." She stopped for a second and wiped at her face, her professional demeanor cracking, taking a deep breath. "Goddamnit, Frank. Tell me you'll get the fuckers that did this."

I opened my mouth to answer but Smith jumped in first. "I thought the assailants were dead?"

"Better I show you," she said.

We walked out of the tent, passed another smaller tent that must have covered Browning. I didn't need to stop and look. I didn't know either agent well, but well enough, and had no desire to see them like this. The ME could tell me everything I needed to know.

At the dunes, we skirted wide so as not to disturb any evidence and scrambled up the shifting sand. From the top, I could see for miles in both directions along the beach. In front of me was the Gulf, and behind was a myriad of scrubland, small bushes, and out in the distance, the National Seashore Park Road. At night it would have been pitch black out here. I'd have to check on how much moonlight there was.

We walked about ten yards along the dunes to another tent similarly set up. We stopped on the periphery of the tent overhang, Doctor Hutchins described what we were looking at.

"The two assailants are dressed only in board shorts, no IDs and from a preliminary check, no tattoos, no scarring, I'll check prints and dental records after I get them back to the morgue. Both of them have multiple gunshot wounds. To the torso, leg, and arm on this one," she pointed, "an arm, leg, and head shot on the other, consistent with the guns the CGIS agents were using, that we found on scene.

"We found footprints leading away from these bodies. It's hard to tell if we are dealing with one individual who left and came back, or someone who came to take a look and ran off, or some other variation. The sand is too muddled to make sense of the tracks and has drifted some, maybe that was done on purpose." She shrugged. "Sorry, I don't have anything else to give you right now." Hutchins looked down and away, muttered, "I know it's not much."

"It's alright, doc," I said. I put my hand on her shoulder for support and waited until we made eye contact. "It's a start." I dropped my hand. "We'll have to work with what we've got. You said these two were all that was up here?"

She nodded.

"And you searched the area, I'm assuming?"

Another nod. "Besides the footprints we didn't find anything."

"So, no bags, no weapons," Carter said. "We're looking for at least one more person. Someone had to have taken the weapons."

"You're right, Jess. The dead guys couldn't have policed their own weapons. So at least one unsub we're looking for. Maybe more."

"Shit," Smith said. "Carter, Dalton, I'm assigning this case to you. Top priority, drop everything else. This case gets your undivided attention until you catch these shitheads. Put out a BOLO to the local PD. It's a long shot as we don't know how many, what we're looking for, or where they're going, but alert them anyway. Maybe they'll pick someone up that'll turn out to be our guys."

Smith turned and walked back down the dunes toward the truck, the weight of the dead agents resting squarely on his shoulders. I looked at Carter.

"I've got this," she said. "You go with him. We'll compare notes later."

I nodded and followed Smith's footprints in the sand to the truck. This was one of the many times I wished I smoked again. We sat in the car with the air conditioning running and the windows down, letting the warm breeze bring in the salt air, while the car cooled it down. Gotta love these government rides and free gas.

"Want me to give you a ride back to the office?" I asked.

Smith stared out of the windshield, silent for a moment. "Mmm, sorry. I was a world...what did you say?"

"I asked if you needed a ride back to the office or your car."

"Yes, sure. Car, thanks. Sorry, I was just thinking. I knew Miner. We used to play racquetball twice a week at the Athletic Club on Staples. He was always beating me. We'd just taken up pickleball, made it seem effortless." Smith turned and looked at me, offering a weak smile. "I'd run around the court like a mad thing, bouncing off the walls and he'd just stand in the middle barely moving, making me do all the work. I have to tell his family, you know. Make the notification to his next of kin. Molly's her name. His wife, I mean. No kids, thankfully. I guess that makes it easier. Browning had three kids, though. Shit."

I didn't say anything. Didn't need to. I just put the truck in drive and headed back down the beach and back to the navy base where we'd left his car. Carter was staying behind so we wouldn't have to wait for the ME's report, and I was going to go back to the office and...and what? I had no clue where to start on this one. The forensics weren't much help so far. So, what did I have? Dead Coasties on a routine patrol along the beach. Dead bad guys dressed in board shorts. Surfers gone bad? No, that was stupid. Okay, so logically the area is known for drug smuggling and illegal migrants, although there are simpler ways to get across the border. So maybe drug smuggling was the connection I should start with. We didn't find any guns or bails or...shit...if they were smuggling drugs, where were the drugs? Did someone take them as well? How many accomplices did they have?

I dropped off Smith back at his car and headed out of the back gate of the base, drove down Ocean Drive, for once not enjoying the view, reached the office and held my badge out to the security guard as I pulled up to the underground parking lot. He gave it a once-over and hit the button to raise the barrier, and as I drove down the darkened ramp, the headlights of the truck came on automatically. I parked in my usual spot, reversing in so it was easier to get out later, and took the stairs instead of the elevator. It wasn't for anything health-related, although I supposed it helped. I just didn't want to wait.

In the office, I nodded to a few people, faces grim and downcast. I grabbed a cup of coffee from the pot and made my way to my desk. It was in the middle of a sea of cubicles, each precisely five foot four, so that when I stood up, I could see from one end of the room to the other. I sat, shoved my ID into the CAC reader on the computer and waited for the, what felt like 1950s speed technology to boot up. The entire world was on Windows version Billion, and we were on what, ME? Number five? All I knew was that it was slow. Might as well have Commodore 64s or Atari's.

The computer booted up, and I logged into MISLE, our law enforcement database. Once that loaded, I put in a few search terms to see if it would spit something out. It was a long shot, and I knew it, and after the computer crunched and, I could have sworn, gurgled and hiccupped a few times, I got the equivalent of a big fat raspberry.

I sipped my coffee and grimaced. It was cold and sour. Maybe we could hire somebody to mess cook and keep the coffee going. It seemed like a simple enough request, hot and fresh coffee. I don't know how the military or anyone else could function without high doses of caffeine. It was about the only legal thing that was left that didn't mark you as a pariah. Those who smoked were looked at like second-class citizens these days. The dipping culture was mostly gone, but I guess a lot of the younger crowd vaped or slammed some cold caffeinated garbage out of a can. It seemed like the only safe place to drink alcohol was in the corner of your garage, with the lights off, by yourself, late at night. The vices weren't gone; they were just forced underground, which was sooo much healthier.

Answer the following questions about your alcohol consumption:

How often do you consume alcohol?

a. daily

b. weekly

c. monthly

d. not at all

Well, d. not at all. Duh.

How many standard drinks do you consume in one sitting when you drink?

a. more than six

b. two to six

c. less than two

d. I rarely consume alcohol, if at all

Pffft. d.

I don't know anyone who tells the truth on the annual health questionnaire.

I inhaled deeply, my chest rising and falling. It wasn't really that bad, but after almost twenty years of service in the Coast Guard, it certainly felt like it sometimes.

I walked to our break room and tipped out my coffee in the sink, emptied the pot, and rummaged around for some filters and grounds. I'd just got it all together when Smith walked in.

"Did you do the next of kin notifications already?" I said.

He shook his head. "No. I know it's chicken shit of me, but I couldn't do it. Not yet. Not until we have something to tell them."

I hesitated, but then dove in. "Tobias, man. I know this sucks ass beyond belief. I knew those guys too, worked out with them, ate with them I...know it's hard...but you can't think of yourself. Even though we—you—even though we're all grieving too. You have to think about the families. They've probably seen the news by now, they know something's up, their loved ones haven't come home yet. Don't leave them hanging."

Smith rubbed his face. "Of course. You're right, Frank. Would you mind?"

I knew what he was asking and didn't hesitate. "Not at all. Let me grab my jacket. Do you have the addresses?"

"Yeah. Neither one lived far."

I didn't want to go with Tobias, but our fallen comrades deserved all the respect we could give them now. I met Smith at the elevator, and we rode down in silence to the parking lot.

Two

"That was shitty, Pete. I never want to do that again," I said. I was saddled up to the bar that my good friend Pete owned. He was also the proprietor, waiter, dishwasher and my old colleague and mentor. His bar also happened to be right across from the T-Heads in downtown Corpus Christi, where I moored my boat, *Serenity*. She used to have a different name, but during that case with Black, he'd sent someone on board and turned it upside down. It had left a bad taste in my mouth, and in a complete break in character for me, on the advice of a friend, I'd used the services of a shaman, of all things, to do her cleansing mojo. I was skeptical, to say the least, but what was the worst thing that could happen? Anyway, turns out she did a great job. The boat felt cleansed but needed a new name. I came up with *Serenity*. Just felt right.

"I never liked having to do next of kin notifications. I don't miss that part of the job for sure. Thankfully, I only had to do it twice. Do you guys have any idea when the funerals will be? I'd like to pay my respects, you know, for old time's sake."

"No idea yet. I don't think the MEs even released the bodies. When Jess gets here, she'll probably have a better idea. She was with Doctor Hutchins all day."

"How are the two of you? I haven't seen you in a while."

"Hutchins? She's fine, I guess." I tried to hide my smirk behind my beer.

"No, you idiot. Jessica. How is your girlfriend?"

Pete was more than just a good friend. He'd helped me find Carter when she'd been kidnapped. He knew what it took for her to get back on her feet afterward. He'd been the manager and owner of this bar—called Pete's, he said it was easier to remember—since he'd gotten out of the Coast Guard. He was my mentor early in my career, showing me what the Coast Guard could be like and should be like, rather than the experiences I'd had at my first unit where pretty much everyone had gone out of their way to be assholes.

When fresh Boots hear horror stories about the 'Old Guard'—and there is some truth to those stories—but like anything else, the dinosaurs and shitheads fade away, and you're left with the people that have touched your soul, people that have made terrible things right. Pete was one of the good ones.

One of the reasons I'd moved *Serenity* to the T-Heads was so that I wouldn't be too far away from him. He'd grown into a big brother of sorts, the only family I had left.

It'd been a few years since his discharge, and although somewhat long in the tooth, he was still in pretty good shape. His black hair was streaked with gray, worn longer than he did when we were in service together, a smudge of stubble on his face, a flex of arm showing strength in his biceps, stomach with a slight curve but nothing a tan couldn't hide.

"We're good," I said, and then shook my head. "Actually, Pete, I don't know. We're not like we were before, you know. But better than could be expected, I guess. Jess still has nightmares. The docs say it's PTSD from her trauma." I shrugged. "I try and help, but she doesn't want to let me in. But I'm here for her, whatever she needs. I'm lucky she's such a strong woman."

"Who's a strong woman," Carter said, an edge to her voice, sitting down next to me at the bar. "You're talking about Wonder Woman, right? 'Cos you wouldn't be talking about me, would you? Can I get a vodka seltzer with a splash of cranberry, please, Pete? Make it a large one."

"Sure thing," he said.

I reached out my hand to her, and she shrank back, flinching. "Jess, I—"

"Don't. Please."

I gave her a minute to herself. Pete put the drink down on the bar in front of her and made himself scarce.

Carter was a different woman from the one I'd fallen in love with. This version of Carter was still her, but she'd been changed by her experiences last year, both physically and emotionally. She'd leaned out, her soft curves gone. Her strength, previously hidden, had turned into hard muscle, more striking and defined, but it had also added an element of harshness, no that wasn't right, maybe toughness was a better word? Anyway, whatever it was, it wasn't there before.

She was determined never to be a victim again. Whichever way you shake it, what happened wasn't her fault. She was kidnapped and drugged. There was nothing anyone could have done to prevent it. No amount of training. But she wanted to be more prepared. Her experience as a federal law enforcement officer had given her more of an edge than most, but she drove herself relentlessly.

She'd returned to her years-long long training in Brazilian Jiu-Jitsu and started training in Krav Maga, arguably two of the hardest and heaviest hitting martial arts. Last month, in an eight-hour competition bout, damn near dropping from exhaustion, she'd slammed down her last opponent to earn her brown belt in BJJ. She'd already earned yellow in Krav Maga.

She was a formidable woman. And while this had shaped her body, her mind was still eggshells. Meditation, exercise, and therapists weren't quite hitting the spot, but I remained hopeful. I stood by her side. Always.

"I'm sorry, Frank," she said, turning to face me after taking a long pull of her drink. "Today has just been really, really, hard. I know Pete was just asking after me, that's what friends do. It just rubbed me the wrong way when I came in, that's all. Look, I'm better now. Okay?" She tried smiling, but it didn't quite reach her eyes.

I studied her for a second. She had dark circles under her unfathomable brown eyes, her auburn hair tied up in a relaxed bun, clasped with a pencil. Some loose-fitting sweats rounded out her ensemble, but it couldn't hide her lithe, taut beauty, even if she was beaten down, tired.

"You look good," I said.

"And that proves you're getting older. You're going blind. How could you see all this," she waved a hand at herself, "and still see beauty? It's not possible." The smile this time was real, the corners of her eyes crinkling ever so slightly, but the smile disappeared as quickly as it had come.

I sighed. "When will you give up and understand that you are beautiful, and you will always be beautiful? It doesn't matter what you say, dress like, or do. You just are. Inside and out." I took a swig of beer and shifted in my chair to face her. "Do you want to talk about today?"

"No," she shook her head. "I want to try and enjoy my drink and do my damnedest to forget about today as much as possible. Tomorrow will come soon enough, and we can deal with all the shit then."

"Fair enough. Let's go home when you're done, then." Home for both of us was *Serenity*. Carter still maintained her apartment downtown, and I'd been asking her when she was going to give it up, save some money. She always deftly avoided the answer.

The next day dawned early, the sunlight smiling through a thin layer of clouds like a gap-toothed child as if to say that nothing wrong had happened the day before. I knew it was a lie, though. Two of my friends and colleagues, brothers in arms, were dead. Gone. But not buried yet. Not yet.

I eased myself out of bed, my back twinging from the movement. I wasn't particularly old—at least that's what I told myself, although some days I felt it more than others. I thought I looked my age, somewhere in my mid-thirties, with perhaps a dash of debonair? A soupçon of modesty? A flash of brilliance? Honestly, I had trouble remembering how old I was most days. It wasn't a number I thought about much.

I felt my rough stubble and wondered if a beard might help the overall look. As an agent, I didn't have to worry about uniforms or grooming standards. We were encouraged to look less like federal agents, if possible, but some of my colleagues had taken that to the extreme, and you'd be forgiven if you mistook them for a homeless person down on their luck.

I went through the morning ritual, making coffee, taking a quick sea shower in my cupboard-sized, onboard bathroom, and drying off with a towel I'd used several times before. Hey, if water is precious, laundry was undoubtedly sacred.

"Hey, babe," I said, nudging Carter. "I'm leaving. What time are you on?"

She rolled over to face me, a smile touching her face, and yawned, her jaw cracking.

"Ouch," I said.

"You heard that?"

I nodded.

"Huh. I must be a little more stressed than I thought."

I gave her a quizzical look.

"My jaw always tenses up when I get stressed. Hasn't happened for..." Her voice trailed off, as the words she said sunk into her consciousness. There was that damn kidnaping rearing its ugly head again. I sat down on the edge of the bed, and hugged her, not saying anything. Nothing needed to be said. We'd done this before.

After a little while, I felt her relax, and I leaned back enough so that I could look at her. "Okay?"

She nodded. "I'm fine. Scooch. I have to use the head."

I got up, giving her some space to get by. "I'm leaving, okay? I'll catch you later," I said through the door of the head. I caught her muffled reply as an affirmative, poured some coffee, and walked off *Serenity* and onto the dock at the T-heads in Corpus.

THREE

The Haqqani network is the terrorist organization nobody ever paid much attention to. At least not in America. But that was about to change.

In the early morning hours, birds still chirping merrily with the rise of the sun, two men strolled slowly along the sidewalk on the bank of San Antonio's River Walk, about a two-hour drive from Corpus Christi. The men had stolen a beat-up Chevy Malibu, hot-wired it, and escaped from the law enforcement net in Corpus. Their mission wasn't in San Antonio, but they needed to put some space between themselves and the incident on the beach. They'd abandoned the vehicle near a homeless camp and set fire to it, assuming rightly the authorities would blame the folks at the camp.

The San Antonio River Walk follows the San Antonio River for about two-and-a-half miles, sitting one story below street level and surrounded by restaurants, shops, hotels, and entertainers. At this time of the morning, the river walk was virtually deserted, absent roving Mariachi bands so prevalent in the evenings, so Alpha and Charlie mostly had the sidewalk to themselves.

"What do we do now?" Charlie said.

"We complete the mission," Alpha replied.

The two men weren't typical jihadists. Including their two deceased brethren, they were all born and raised in America. White-skinned and of fair complexion. They all came from different backgrounds. Alpha had grown up on the

Connecticut Gold Coast, an affluent area in the southwest of the state, not too far from New York City. He'd gone to all the right schools. Had both, albeit emotionally distant, but still caring, parents. And had the right connections and tools to set him up for a lifetime of success. But as often happens with kids, privileged or not, he thought he knew better than most. And then in college he met a girl called Tasmin.

Alpha, whose real name was Alexander Winthrop III, fell head over heels for Tasmin. She was a wild child and rebelled against the establishment—not seeing the irony in the fact that it was because of the establishment her parents could afford to pay for her school—and often went to protests, particularly ones where America was being, 'beastly abroad,' as she put it one night to Winthrop.

"It's true, Alex," Tasmin said. "You should see the awful atrocities they're perpetuating in the Middle East. This war must stop, we've been invaders in Afghanistan for decades now, no different than the Russians or British. It. Has. To. Stop." Tasmin stamped her foot in time with her words.

Winthrop didn't really care what America was doing overseas, but if it was important to Tasmin, then it was important to him.

"Did you see what they just did? What we just did, America I mean? It was all over the news," she said.

Winthrop shook his head. He didn't care for the news.

"They released one of those awful bombs, a MOAB they called it on the news, the Mother Of All Bombs, if you can believe that. It landed in some place called Nangarhar Province in Afghanistan." She leaned closer to Winthrop and lowered her voice. "The news said it was released to try and get the leader of some," Tasmin air quoted, "terrorist group. Some people, they said, called the Haqqani network. I've never heard of them, have you?"

Winthrop dutifully shook his head again.

"Didn't think so." Tasmin looked around before she said the next part, settling it in her head. "I think they made it up. The news said the bomb was a success, but I saw other news, stuff they don't want you to see, I saw the bomb landed on a school, killing tons of kids. Innocents."

Winthrop made sure he looked appropriately shocked.

"They're having a protest about it later. Banners and everything. Do you want to come?"

Winthrop didn't. But he ended up going. Because of Tasmin.

Back in San Antonio, Charlie continued to be worried. "How can we complete the mission? Bravo and Delta are dead," he said, stopping and turning to face Alpha, his arm on Alpha's shoulder.

Alpha reached up and patted Charlie's arm and then gently pushed it from his shoulder. "Because we must, my friend. The mission continues. Just because our friends died on the battlefield does not mean we give up. No, it makes our mission even more vital. We were sent here to make America wake up, to realize what harm they're doing to the rest of the world. The American public must be shown that we need to look after ourselves first. Protect our borders, help our hungry and homeless. What happens on the other side of the world is not our business. America must come first."

Charlie sighed. "I know all that, man. And I don't disagree with you, I'm just saying with two of our team gone, I don't know if we can complete our mission."

Charlie hadn't had a privileged upbringing like Alpha; in fact, it couldn't have been more different. Charlie came from a broken home. His dad had left the family before Charlie could even talk and never came back. His mother, struggling for money, had ended up getting married again, but this time to an even bigger deadbeat. With his mother working all the time and his dead-beat stepfather drinking and watching TV, Charlie's parental guidance was nonexistent, and he fell in with the wrong crowd. In and out of juvie, his hatred of the system grew.

The MOAB Tasmin was upset about was dropped in the mountainous range of the Wazir Tanki District in the Nangarhar Province in Afghanistan, near the border of Pakistan. This was the Haqqani network stronghold. The goal was to wipe out the stronghold of one Maulvi Jalaluddin Haqqani and his son, Sirajuddin Haqqani, who together ran the terrorist group.

Through much congratulatory backslapping, the US officials celebrated another successful mission and were certain maximum devastation had occurred.

From the satellite photos came images of underground cave-ins and no movement of people, and from this limited data they declared the mission a success.

They were wrong. Their Humint or human intelligence on the ground had gotten it wrong, and the leaders weren't on location. It didn't, however, stop the Haqqani from pushing out images of dying children, which were quickly spread around the world. The images weren't fake, they were just of a different attack, this one perpetrated by the Haqqani network jihadists but now attributed to America instead.

"Our mission was to block shipping lanes," Alpha said. "Bring America to its knees. Cripple commerce, cripple the economy. Create fear."

"I know what the mission was, I'm saying with half our team gone, we have to reassess, maybe we can pick different targets."

"Listen, Charlie," he said, looking around and leaning in. "I don't know for sure what the grand plan was or is, but you know everything's compartmentalized. I can't imagine we're the only team that got into the US, but even if we are, we must complete the mission. If we do anything less than that, it's just bullshit. All of this for nothing. Bravo and Delta's deaths meaningless." He straightened up. "We do what we were trained for and pray that the other teams do the same."

Charlie ran a hand through his hair and gestured with the other in frustration. "I want those bastards on the beach to pay. I care about the mission, but I care about payback even more. Why can't we do the mission after."

"And how's that going to work, huh?" Alpha said, stepping back and raising his voice slightly. "We already killed those two on the beach. What's your payback gonna look like? Take out a couple more Coast Guard people? Blow up a shitty small boat? Then what? We just saunter around and finish the real mission? Get real. We probably already have every law enforcement agency on red alert, looking for the boogie man. The only good thing is they don't know how many of us there are, or what we look like or what we're planning on doing. If we start blowing up half the fucking Coast Guard, we're gonna get caught." Alpha looked up and down the sidewalk, his gaze lingering for a moment on an old man on the other side of the river shuffling along. Once he deemed him a non-threat, he looked back to Charlie. "Let's keep moving, we can discuss this when we're on the road. Either way, we need to get back to Corpus."

Alpha never intended to become a terrorist, nor did Charlie. Alpha became bitter and disillusioned with America during another protest that Tasmin had dragged Winthrop to. This time in support of a free Palestine.

"Come on, Alex. This is the only way the world will know it's not okay. We must show our support for Palestine and our disapproval of the way Israel are doing things. I mean, I like the people, don't get me wrong, I just don't like how their government are slaughtering people."

If Winthrop did have an opinion on the matter, it was long gone, having been systematically overruled by Tasmin's opinions. Winthrop had been to so many of these protests since he'd been dating Tasmin that they all kind of blended together, but this one was to stick in his head for quite some time and spurred his transition from all around American Alexander Winthrop III to the terrorist Alpha, committed to make America feel threatened and to turn introspective. America first.

The inaugural cruise of the sixty-five-thousand-ton cruise ship *Nexus Joy* left the port of New Orleans in Louisiana, with much fanfare, fireworks, banners, and general joviality. Waitstaff on the lido deck served complimentary champagne and canapés—nothing was as tacky as 'free' on the *Nexus Joy*, but plenty was complimentary. Photographers on the promenade deck gently cajoled passengers—guests—to turn around and have a flattering photo taken with the skyline of New Orleans in the background. The cruise director entertained guests with witty repartee while a legion of cooks—chefs—prepared delicate morsels of delight for their guests' discerning palates. Nothing was left to chance; nothing was left to ambiguity. Everything was planned, developed, rehearsed, and perfect.

The ship, although brand new, was small by today's standards, but was built to offer an alternative to the megalithic-sized, five and six thousand passenger, fifteen hundred crew, cruise ships full of screaming, drunken hordes. This was an exclusive ship. Passengers were hand-selected and invited. There were no discounts, drinks were premium, and world-renowned chefs cooked the food. Nothing was cheap, and it wasn't meant to be. If you expected your five-dollar drink to cost twenty, it was accepted. If it were cheap, it would just scream budget. The *Nexus Joy* was anything but budget; it was a cozy chalet of eight hundred, hosted by an unheard of passenger to crew ratio of one to one.

The captain, a beefy, broad Norwegian with hairy hands the size of ham hocks and thirty years of an unblemished sailing record under his belt, was in charge. He gazed out of the bridge windows as the ship maneuvered successfully and seamlessly away from the dock. After so many years at sea, one could be forgiven for thinking that the captain was past his prime, or perhaps weary of the constant sea-time. That person would be wrong. The crew, just like the guests, had been hand-selected and plucked from other positions and offered a superbly lucrative, competitive package to sail aboard the *Nexus Joy*. The crew, from the lowliest cabin—stateroom—cleaner or bilge rat, on up to the captain, was just as equally excited and pleased to be on board.

The itinerary was to be different too. From New Orleans they would sail to Sanibel Island and Key West in Florida and then to Costa Maya, Mexico, before heading to Corpus Christi, a destination of beaches, easy access to San Antonio and the Alamo. It wasn't an itinerary that made sense in the traditional circular routes; the *Nexus Joy* was trying to do something a little different, a little quirky, a lot expensive. Corpus Christi may not have sounded like a particularly exciting destination, but the Port Authority had gone all out, building a new terminal next to the aquarium. Corpus had been trying to attract cruise ships for years, competing with the nearby hub of Galveston, literally a few hours' drive along the coast. Because of the *Nexus Joy's* size, Corpus could offer premium facilities, and as no other cruise ships currently docked there, the *Nexus Joy* could advertise this exclusivity, perhaps temporarily, but with abandon.

The beginning of the transition from Alexander Winthrop III, upstanding student, to Alpha the terrorist was during the last protest march he went to with Tasmin. She'd perhaps been a little more vocal than usual, and perhaps the police in their riot gear had been a little more forceful than usual. But in the end the result was the same. Tasmin never recovered from a head injury she sustained after being hurt at the protest. Winthrop only knew that the catalyst for the injury was Tasmin falling to the ground after being pushed back by a wall of riot shields, manned by perhaps overzealous officers. What would never be known was how Tasmin sustained her head injury. Was it from the strike of a riot shield? From the fall to the ground? From a boot hitting her in the head in the melee that followed? No one would ever know. CCTV footage was useless, no one came forward with cell phone coverage, and the officers' body cams had developed a glitch around that time.

All that Winthrop knew was that Tasmin never recovered, and as time went on, he blamed the establishment more and more. By the time the inquest into Tasmin's death was over he was ready to lash out.

It could have been any organization that Winthrop latched onto but because the MOAB was aimed at the Haqqani and because that was Tasmin's last protest, Winthrop felt it was fate that led him there. The Haqqani network supports international jihadists. Their aim to rout out Western influence worldwide and destroy it. And while Winthrop didn't consider himself a jihadist, for the time being their goals aligned albeit with different motives.

Alpha, Bravo, Charlie and Delta, unknown to each other at the time, made their circuitous way to Afghanistan. They used standard US passports to travel out of the country as they were not on any watchlist. Flights to France, Germany, and Spain, from there to Africa, Morocco, Egypt and Sudan, flights to Pakistan, and the border through to Afghanistan.

If America had kept to itself, hadn't cajoled and complained and interfered with other nations, Tasmin wouldn't have been at that protest. And she'd still be with Winthrop. That's what Winthrop believed. Although in truth, Tasmin was the type of girl who would have found something else to protest about.

Of course, it wasn't that easy to just find a terrorist cell, say hello, I'm a disillusioned American, could you please train me in insurgency techniques, bomb making and everything else. Indeed, with the shaky knowledge each man had, it was a surprise they found anyone at all. And with good reason. If these four could just stroll in, what would stop a SEAL team?

So, there were checks and balances. False drops, meets, demands to be met, money had to pass hands, but eventually the four men found their way. Even then, the Haqqani network did not welcome the four Americans warmly. They were beaten and tortured. Bags placed on their heads and then thrown into dank, dark caves. No food, only a little water every few days. And subjected to readings from the Koran, the passages bastardized by the terrorists to promote their own jihadist cause. They would teach these infidels.

Day by day, month after month, the soul weaker, nerves shattered, the body frail, they converted.

Radicalized.

Learned to hate America. Although Alpha and Charlie already had a deep burning hatred of the system.

Allahu Akbar. Allah is Greater, often misquoted in the media as God is great, sang from broken streets.

In truth, the Haqqani network didn't really care what these infidels believed. It was enough for the Haqqani trainers to point the four men in the right direction and see what happened.

FOUR

It was a short drive to the office from the T-heads. There were rumors we were finally going to be moving to the new building by the commercial airport. They'd started building, but then, like all things' government, the construction had ground to a halt when the Coast Guard defaulted on the loan. No money. No budget. Continuing resolution, the President threatening to defund us. We were the smallest service, with some of the toughest jobs. The other services trained every day for events they hoped would never happen. The Coast Guard did their job every day because it did happen, and I did mine. There was little enough time for practice. Maybe I could get them to remove the dunker training? I doubt if I were ever in a helicopter crash, it was going to be as nice as being upside down in a heated pool. It was inevitable that it would happen, moving to the new building, that is, but it wouldn't be this week.

At work, I checked in with new Mark at the DOMEX digital forensics lab. Last year, someone murdered the original Mark for trying to help me with that Black case. I'd asked Mark to do some research for me, never really considering that would put him in danger. He'd been murdered in a coffee shop head practically right under my nose. I didn't kill him, but if it weren't for me asking, he wouldn't have been there, so I blame myself.

Anyway, I still felt terrible about it, so I hadn't bothered to learn the new guy's name, merely calling him new Mark. I know it wasn't fair, but he didn't seem to mind, although I'd never asked him. Maybe it was time for me to stop being such an asshole.

"What have you got for me?" I said when I walked in. The lab hasn't changed much in the last year. I guess when you have a fully functioning forensics lab, where the smallest instrument costs hundreds of thousands of dollars, there wasn't much need for any change. That and the old budget chestnut again. You could probably build one of those fancy new Coast Guard cutters with all the money in this room. Thank God that the powers that be realized that to compete with the bad guys in this world we needed cutting-edge tech. In fact, most of this stuff rivaled what the FBI and major crime labs had, although we only had three DOMEX facilities in the country.

"Agent," said new Mark, "nothing on the case unfortunately, but may I express my condolences for the loss of the agents. I...I never knew them personally, but it was a tragic, senseless loss. Anything I can do here, to help, you've got it."

I muttered my thanks and went to find some coffee. I needed to get my head together to see if I could come up with a direction to head this investigation in. I found some coffee and sat at my desk, staring at the computer monitor. I don't know how long I'd been like that, zoned out, but I jumped when Carter yelled at me.

"Frank!"

"What's up?"

"Where were you? I've been talking to you for ages."

"I was right here." I took a swig of the coffee I'd just made. Ugh. Cold. I looked at my watch and was shocked to discover it was almost lunchtime. What the...I jiggled the mouse on the computer, waking the screen, and realized I'd never even got my CAC out to log on. Where had I been?

"Not sure," I finally answered Carter. "I got coffee, sat down...And then the next thing I know is you're yelling at me. I must have really zoned out."

Carter frowned. "That's not normal, Frank."

I nodded. "Sure." I changed the subject. "Where are we at on the investigation? Heard from Doctor Hutchins yet?"

"I was just about to call her, but we could drive over if you need a breath of fresh air."

I considered that for a moment and then said, "Sure. Probably be good to stretch my legs. Let me grab my jacket and use the head and I'll meet you in the parking lot."

On the drive over to the morgue, where Doctor Hutchins, the medical examiner worked, I thought about asking Carter what was up. I'd definitely noticed a change in her. She was more withdrawn, snappier, if that was a good way to describe someone. Perhaps more on edge would be a better description. I shrugged inwardly and glanced over at her. She was staring out the window of the truck, and my breath hitched for a second. She looked sad. I must have been louder than I thought.

Carter turned to me. "Yeah?"

"Hmmm. Nothing. Was just thinking about this case, is all," I said, preferring not to talk it out and wallow in my own insecurities.

"Right," she said. "Me too."

Now it was my turn to look at her. Of course the case was important, but was that really what she was thinking as she looked out the window? Either way, we'd both ignored whatever it was.

I parked the car in the MEs parking lot, braced for the Corpus heat as I got out of the truck, already sweating by the time I got to the door of the morgue, and held the door open for Carter as the strong air conditioning immediately cooled me.

"Doc, what have you got," I said, breezing through the double doors, Carter right behind me.

Dressed in scrubs and masked up, she looked up from what she was doing and nodded at us. Moving over to the sink, she pulled off her blue nitrile gloves, washed her hands for a good minute while we just stood there watching, dried her hands and pulled her mask down.

She gave us a weak smile. "Hi guys. Not a lot I'm afraid, besides confirming my preliminary findings on the beach. Both agents were shot with high velocity

9mm rounds. Judging by the wounds I would say you're looking for some sort of machine pistol rather than a regular piece."

I nodded. "Any idea on the shooters?"

She shook her head. "Actually, yes. The CSI guys worked through the night on the bullet fragments we recovered and found four distinct sets of bullets based on the rifling, you know the striations each weapon produces, almost as good as a fingerprint."

That was something. "So, four shooters?"

"I believe so, yes. I wouldn't swear to it in a court of law, and of course, there's always the chance there were more weapons than people or more people than guns." She shrugged. "But, of course you're the investigator."

I pondered that. Carter looked at me and shrugged. Could be four people. With two dead, could it be that we were only looking for two more? I'll take those odds.

"Okay. Anything else?"

"The CSI team have also partially finished processing the agents' SUV. So far, they've analyzed all the prints from the vehicle and Browning and Miner's were the only prints they found. I should be able to give you a firmer grasp of the order of events later today or tomorrow morning. I've put a rush on the tox screening, and that should come back tomorrow as well, although I don't expect any surprises. At least from our guys."

"What about the dead perps? Anything you can tell me about them, where they came from, who they are?"

She shrugged again. "I'm sorry Frank, I feel like a broken record. Not a lot. Both white males, mid to late twenties, no distinguishing marks, appear to be physically fit, decent muscle mass, no signs of malnutrition. They both died from multiple gunshot wounds consistent with the weapons the agents had at the scene. I've sent casts of the dental records out and I'm running the fingerprints through CODIS, but as you know, if they don't have a record or haven't been printed, they won't show up. I'm hopeful for the dental records as it's almost impossible to go through life without dental work, but, and here's a big but, if they're not from the US, then that will take considerably longer to get any results."

I walked over to Hutchins and gave her a hug. She almost collapsed in my arms. "It's okay, doc. Thank you for what you've done so far."

"It's so hard, Frank. I knew these guys." Her breath hitched, and she pulled away, wiping a tear on the sleeve of her lab coat. "Tell me again, you'll get these fuckers?"

"We will," Carter and I said in unison.

We left the morgue and headed back to the office. "Late lunch?" I said to Carter. "I know a good place—"

Carter glanced at me, and I saw a whisper of a polite smile. "I'm good, thanks. I've got a few things I need to take care of before the end of the day."

And we drove back to the office in silence.

I went through the motions at the office, but with no new leads, nothing yet from the ME or follow on from the CSI guys, there wasn't a lot to go on. I looked for Smith, but he didn't have anything either, and neither did new Mark.

I needed to do something, although there was nothing to do. Frustrated, I decided to take a drive out to North Padre Island to take another look at the crime scene before it got dark. Maybe there was something we missed.

FIVE

"Hey boss, we've got a silent alarm pinging downtown," the watch officer for Sledge Security said. She was a small redhead who wore wire-framed glasses, even though she didn't need them. All about fashion, you know? And skirts. Skirts were important. Skirts that were also excessively short for the night shift. But that was her thing, and it wasn't like this was a public office, so who cared? It wasn't like there was a dress code or anything.

"Where?" asked the supervisor. She had little love for the watch officer. It wasn't so much her job performance, which was exemplary, but her firm, young skin, her perkiness, and the fact that gravity wasn't as unkind to her as she felt it should have been. As unfair as it was to herself.

The watch officer pulled up a detailed map on her screen. "It's coming from 555 North Carancahua Street. Looks like Tower Two. The door from the parking garage alarmed."

"Alright. It's probably just someone who tried to use an expired access code or something. Better send a car over to check it out anyway. Who's on call?"

The watch officer consulted the online scheduling calendar, zeroing on the graveyard shift, looking through her fake glasses. "Looks like Arnie Geller's on tonight."

"Well, fuck. Of course he is. There's no one else?"

"He's the only patrol within ten miles."

Arnie was a nice enough guy. He had a few extra pounds around the middle—well, if she was honest with herself, it was more than a few—but that didn't matter so much. Hell, I could do with losing a few pounds myself, she thought. No, it wasn't the weight. Arnie was just the tiniest bit on the wrong side of creepy. Always making weird jokes no one ever gets, putting up a front of indignation whenever anyone joked about him. Whatever that was about.

The watch supervisor pulled the mike closer from the dispatch desk. "Geller, control. Come in," she said.

A few moments later, the radio crackled to life, and a tinny voice came through. "Go for Geller." The go was long and drawn out.

She sighed at his idiotic radio language. "Geller, check out Tower Two downtown. The parking garage access door to the main building just alarmed on the east side."

There was some static on the line when he replied. "Confirmed. En route Tower Two."

"Geller, what's that noise? You eating Doritos again on company time?" It was a stupid comment, one that wasn't needed, but it made her feel better in the middle of the night.

"Err. That's a negative, control."

"Roger. Oh, and make sure you turn on your body cam when you get there. Control, out." The body cam was a new feature for Sledge Security.

Geller arrived downtown a few minutes later and parked in the underground lot adjacent to Tower Two. As he walked, he absentmindedly brushed bright orange crumbs off his uniform shirt and sucked his fingers clean, smacking his lips.

He'd spoken with the security guard on duty at the entrance ramp on the way in, but he said he hadn't seen anything all night. Geller doubted he would have noticed the Spanish Armada if it had floated by. He fumbled with the on switch of his body cam as he walked. He wasn't a big fan of this new addition, but he supposed it was for his protection as much as anything.

A discrete red light on the front of the unit blinked, indicating it was functioning and recording. His steps echoed around the mostly empty concrete parking lot. He held his flashlight and shone it into the shadows, scaring away the rats gnawing on yesterday's trash and causing the roosting pigeons to flutter and coo.

A fall cold front was visiting, just for a few days, dipping the nighttime temperatures into the low seventies and had lessened the humidity. Even so, Geller was working up a sweat. His underarms moist, the telltale spreading stain glimpsed every time he swung his arms, his face beading with moisture. Geller wiped away the sweat with his shirtsleeve as he rounded the last corner and saw the door that was causing all the trouble and interrupting his snack time.

He shone his light on the security access pad and then at the door. The door had a silent alarm, so any intruders would be unaware if they triggered it.

"Control, this is Geller. I'm on scene. Nothing unusual to report. I'm going to access the building and look around."

"Roger. We'll be here."

Geller swiped his Sledge Security card through the reader, and the door unlatched and buzzed. He pulled it open quickly and moved into the hallway beyond the door. The strip lights in the ceiling buzzed and cast garish shadows onto the floor as he ambled towards the main building, moving in time to his own beat.

He made his way to the lobby and shone his light around. The lobby shouldn't have been this dark. Several lights in the ceiling should be on, providing a subdued nighttime experience, but enough to navigate by. Geller either didn't know this or didn't think it curious that most of the lights were out. He found the elevator and cursed. "How am I supposed to search through this whole place? There're sixteen floors." He keyed his radio. "Control, this is Geller. I'm in the main lobby of the building. There's nothing to see here. I'm going back to the car. The—"

The elevator dinged behind Gellar, so he turned to face it and noticed the floor indicator lighting up, indicating movement from the tenth floor down to the fifth, and staying there.

"Hold on control. I think there's someone on the fifth floor. I'm going to investigate," he said into the radio.

It briefly crossed his mind to take the stairs so he wouldn't give away his position, but he quickly decided against it. It was five floors, and he was already sweating. No use in giving myself a heart attack, he thought. So he hit the call button on the elevator panel. The elevator slid down to the lobby, chimed and opened. Geller stepped in and hit the button for the fifth floor. The doors closed, the elevator jerked and started to ascend.

It slowed as it neared the fifth floor, chimed again, stopped, and the doors slid open. This level held the local Coast Guard prevention offices, the Coast Guard Investigative Service, Customs and Border Patrol, and IRS investigations. Geller moved from one door to the next, shining his light through the glass of the office doors, and rattling the doorknobs to ensure they were closed. This floor was dark too. Again, Geller didn't notice.

As he pushed against the door to the Coast Guard prevention office, it swung open, and Geller stumbled into the foyer, unprepared for its sudden opening as all the other doors were locked.

"What the fu—"

Geller didn't get to finish his sentence. When he stumbled through the doorway, he landed against a man. The man didn't move out of the way but instead thrust his arm into Geller's abdomen. Geller looked down, opening and closing his mouth a few times. He knew on some level something terrible had just happened, but this event was so incongruous and out of his normal element he couldn't string his thoughts together.

He ineffectually tugged at the man's hand, but with his rapidly weakening system he couldn't overcome the stranger and the fact that he'd just been stabbed.

The man twisted the blade and sliced upwards as he pulled it out. It cut through Geller's blubber and internal organs with ease and made a small sucking sound as it came out.

Geller's blood gushed out onto the floor. Several small pieces of vital human machinery followed and splattered onto his shoes. If I had a bucket, Geller thought, I could save all this and donate it. For a last thought, it wasn't very creative or coherent, but then again, it was a last thought. Geller slid to his knees, collapsing unceremoniously to the floor. The final sound was of his head smacking the thin carpet.

The man kneeled and wiped his knife on the sleeve of Geller's uniform. He failed to notice the small blinking light of Geller's body cam still recording.

Six

The cause of the explosion that rocked Tower Two in downtown Corpus Christi wasn't immediately apparent. It was clear the windows on the fifth floor that had once looked out on the Sparkling City by the Sea were now shattered and lying in the street below, but anything beyond that was merely speculation.

Thick black smoke continued to escape from the broken fifth-floor windows, beaten back by firemen on ladder trucks laying down wave after wave of pressurized water to prevent the fire from spreading beyond the fifth floor. On the ground, a small crowd of onlookers had gathered and watched the drama, even at this late hour. Most of them didn't know that this floor held a Coast Guard office; even fewer knew that it also contained the local Coast Guard Investigative Service Agents and other law enforcement agencies.

The building itself also held the offices of various high-priced lawyers and investment firms and, in the basement, several small restaurants where excellent breakfast tacos could be had.

Initial gossip on the street and by the local CBS affiliate Action 10 News broadcasting live on location, suggested this was most likely a gas explosion. The story regurgitated throughout the night until pundits brought on as talking heads to propel ratings for the morning news suggested it could also have been an attack against the IRS. With the fire now out, and the smoke dissipated, the news replayed the dramatic scene from the night before. A member of the public looking to claim his fifteen minutes had captured shaky footage of the actual explosion, which was also played as an exclusive. The IRS story continued to get some play throughout the day. The media, for lack of any facts, wrote their own narrative. After all, everybody hated the IRS, and it was definitely plausible.

As is the case with a slow news day, the story was picked up as breaking news on every major network in America. Who didn't like a juicy story about the taxman?

By the time the lunchtime news anchors were airing, the narrative had already subtly changed. Questions and the inevitable accusations started. An anonymous leak at the fire department suggested the fire was concentrated in the Coast Guard offices. This stumped the media for a moment as they wanted to believe the IRS story, but if this explosion wasn't an accident, why would anyone destroy a Coast Guard office? The Marines or Army, sure, they fought wars, killed terrorists, invaded countries. But the Coast Guard? All they did was search and rescue, right?

It didn't take long to link this explosion with the deaths of the Coast Guard agents on the beach.

Production staff quickly wheeled more talking heads into the studio. Retired one-star admirals looking for publicity and a quick, fat paycheck expounded on the Coast Guard's activities abroad and at home. Alien interdiction, drug smuggling, border security along with port security, radiation detection, overseas boardings, and port blockades and embargoes were bandied about on the news. No one knew the real reason, although many had theories.

Angry exclamations in Washington, D.C. from posturing congressmen and senators, expressing outrage that something like this could happen on US soil made for even better ratings. Most of the time, the government was only too happy to slash the Coast Guard's budget—do more with less—but you had to look the part, right? Moral outrage, whether manufactured or real, was always good for ratings and votes and ensured a primetime soundbite.

I muted the television and let the remote clatter to the table in disgust. "This is just bullshit, Tobias. We should be out there trying to figure out who these assholes were that blew us up, not sitting here with our thumbs up each other's asses."

"Speak for yourself, Frank. My thumb is exactly where it needs to be." We were sitting in a room at the recently stood-up command post at Naval Station Corpus Christi, in Hangar 41, where Coast Guard Sector Corpus Christi had its main command and flight operations. Smith turned and looked at me. "It has nothing to do with being excluded. The fire department arson investigators are sifting through the rubble. ATF is on scene, so is the FBI. There's nothing more we can really add, it's not our ball game. Once they figure out what happened, or have some clues—"

"The ATF and FBI will run with the clues themselves. Come on, Tobias. They're not going to let us run an investigation into a bombing if that's even what it was. They'll wrap it all up, say hey guys, we're all done, you can come clean up now. Maybe get some new windows and an air-freshener.

"Just because we were the target, isn't going to change how they perceive us. Hell, half of them probably don't even know we're part of the Armed Services. No, I stand by what I said. This is just bullshit. It must have something to do with the attack on the beach. Maybe this was retaliation or something."

"Retaliation? Now look who's stretching. I know you want answers, Frank. We all do. Just let them do their jobs."

I turned and looked as the door opened, and Carter walked in. "Jess. Any word?" I said.

"I might have something," she said. "Remember Jim London, the arson investigator that was on Rivas's case last year?"

"Yes, of course. He let us know she was still alive after we thought she was a crispy critter." Rivas, nice lady that she was, had unfortunately been the target of an arson attack by Black.

"Right. Well, he's the lead investigator on this case. He gave me a heads up that something wasn't quite right."

"Let's roll," I said, getting up from my seat.

"Now, hold on a second," Smith said. "Didn't you hear what I said about us not being part of the investigation?"

"I heard you, Tobias. We're not going to interfere, we're just going to have a chat with a colleague. Isn't that right, Agent Carter?"

"That's how I understand it, Agent Dalton," Carter said.

"You two are exasperating. Get out of here. And for Christ's sake don't get in the way. The last thing I need right now is someone up my ass complaining about you two."

"You won't even hear a mouse peep. Seriously."

We walked outside to my truck and drove out the back gate of the Navy base that ran straight onto Ocean Drive. The sea was glittering, and I rolled the windows down, letting the AC buffet me along with the humid sea air. I watched students from Texas A&M University roll into classes as we passed.

It was getting hot already, but it was October and still beautiful without being oppressive. Queen palm trees, fronds ruffling in the wind, dotted the landscape. I watched a group of kite surfers race along the edge of the bay. It was always blowing about fifteen knots in Corpus, so it was ideal for every wind sport you could imagine. I'd even seen kids in parking lots using a bed sheet as a sail to boost them along on their skateboards. It looked like fun.

"Where is London anyway?" I asked Carter.

"Tower Two. He said it was okay if we swung by."

We parked in the underground lot and wedged ourselves between a row of large black SUVs that screamed FBI and ATF and got out. The elevator wasn't working. No doubt the power had been secured, so we hiked up the stairs to the fifth floor. The emergency stairwell lights were on, but when we pushed the fire door open onto the fifth floor, it was dark. I switched on my flashlight, Carter doing the same.

"It freakin' reeks in here," she said.

"What did you expect, the whole place almost burned down."

"I dunno. I wasn't thinking anything." She shrugged. "Maybe like I remembered though, not like this. It's so sad."

Broken glass crunched under our boots as we moved from the elevator, my flashlight bouncing around on scorched walls. The darkness and puddles of water from the fire department made it appear we were spelunking and not walking around the lobby area of our old office.

"Where's London?" I asked.

"I don't know. He just said the fifth floor. Let's walk around a bit. You never know, we might find a clue."

"I could write what I know about fire investigation on your left hand."

"My hand?"

"Yeah. It's smaller than mine. I don't have that much to write."

"Gotcha."

We walked around a bit, careful of where we stepped. Not so much to preserve evidence, but so we wouldn't get our feet wet. As we were passing the Sector Prevention office door, London came out. He was wearing a pair of white Tyvek coveralls, gloves, and a hard hat. Attached to the hard hat was a light.

"Hey, you two. You know you should be in PPE and wearing a hard hat." He tapped his head for emphasis.

"Sorry," I said, chagrined. I shrugged. "We were in a hurry to meet with you."

He huffed a little, and then said, "Fine, there's really nothing I can show you up here that would make any sense, anyway, why don't we go back outside. I have to get a couple of things from my car. We can talk then."

We followed him back down the way we had just come to the underground parking lot and over to a red SUV emblazoned with Corpus Christi Fire Department on the side. He opened the trunk and sat down to pull his Tyvek suit off.

"Sure this is safe down here?" I said. "You know, what with the fire up there and everything."

"Structurally the building is fine," London said. "Honestly, it's mostly cosmetic. You'll need to gut the place, but it won't fall down."

"Well, that's good to know. So, how've you been, Jim?" I said.

London pulled off his gloves, and we shook hands. "Not so bad. Looks like you two are keeping me in business. You wouldn't have any idea who could have done this do you?"

"I was hoping to ask you the same question," Carter said, shaking hands with London.

We all looked at each other for a moment and watched what had to be an FBI agent get into his car. He was dressed in the obligatory black suit, white shirt, and sunglasses. Even down here, where there was no sun. I guess you can take a federal agent out of the building, but you can't take...or whatever that saying was. I watched him drive off in one of the big black SUVs and turned back to London. He'd finished taking off his Tyvek suit and was wearing a pair of fire department coveralls underneath.

"Well, there's not much to go on at the moment. We know something exploded, and it exploded from inside the building on the fifth floor. I can't tell yet if it was an accident or if it was intentional."

"But the news said it was an explosion, or firebomb or whatever."

"That's the media for you." He looked around, even though we were alone. "They don't know shit. Makes a good story if it's not something mundane. Anyway, there's a ton of debris, and some of the frames and longitudinals have been damaged. Like I said it's not really structural, but I can tell you the repairs are going to take months."

Well shit. I didn't feel much like working out of the air station all that time. "Okay. Any clues, sneaking suppositions?"

London smiled. "Perhaps. Give me a minute to load these photos," he waggled a camera in his hand, "onto my laptop and I can show you what I was looking at."

SEVEN

The Coast Guard Cutter *Glorious* had been on patrol for three weeks in the Gulf of Mexico when Captain Carroll heard his name piped over the loudspeaker.

"Now, Captain Carroll your presence is requested on the bridge, now captain to the bridge."

Captain Carroll was a trim man in his early forties. He prided himself on the fact that he could still beat most of his crew, some over twenty years younger than him, in a mile and a half run, the standard fitness test length in the Coast Guard. He took the ladder two steps at a time and was on the bridge within a couple of minutes of being piped.

"Attention on deck!" shouted a seaman as the captain entered.

Almost as soon as the bridge crew jumped to attention, Carroll said, "As you were."

He looked around the bridge for the operations officer and walked over to him.

"OPS, what have you got for me?"

"Good morning, captain. The helo," Lieutenant Junior Grade Peters said, "reported in that they've found the go-fast we've been looking for. It's not responding to any radio calls to stand down, and the pilot is requesting permission to fire disabling shots."

"Are there any other vessels in the area that could be in the line of fire?" Carroll asked.

"No, sir."

The *Glorious* was on patrol explicitly looking for this go-fast. The low-profile boat was a relatively new cartel concept. The boat was low in the water with barely two feet of freeboard and a length of around one hundred and twenty feet. The vessels were specially built for the cartels to run drugs. It was basically two massive gasoline engines and storage space. There were no amenities. Alto su barco.

The Coast Guard had gotten smarter over the years with newer and better equipment. But as they had improved, so had the cartels. It was a cat-and-mouse game. The cartels built super-fast and long speedboats colloquially called go-fasts that could outrun most Coast Guard Cutters. So, the Coast Guard deployed their own speedboats. Then the cartels designed submersible craft and semi-submersible craft. The Coast Guard deployed helicopters with thermal imaging to pick up heat signatures and specially equipped helicopters with snipers on board called HITRON units.

The idea though, that one cutter could look for one very hard to find and camouflaged go-fast in all the Gulf of Mexico was almost laughable, save for the fact that it wasn't a needle in a haystack situation.

A third-class petty officer had been approached by a beautiful woman one night a few weeks back in his local bar. They struck up a conversation and, of course, he told her what he did for a living. She seemed thrilled and asked him if he could get her a Coast Guard hat. She'd pay for it of course. Anyone can get a Coast Guard hat, he thought. They sell them on Amazon, so he agreed.

The next time they met up, she paid him fifty dollars for the hat, although it was only worth fifteen at the most. He protested, but she insisted, seeming upset that he would be so rude, so he acquiesced. Later that week when they met again, she asked him for a Coast Guard sweatshirt. Again, he thought there was no harm in it, and presented it to her the next day. This time she paid him a hundred dollars when it was only worth forty.

About this time, this young petty officer caught on that something wasn't quite right and contacted the Coast Guard's Office of Counterintelligence and reported what was going on. The agent he spoke to agreed to meet him, and after some back and forth, encouraged the relationship. Soon she was asking for detailed plans of this building or that and when the *Glorious* would be on patrol and where. Under the tutelage and guidance of the agent, he fed her false information.

And so, the *Glorious* put to sea, patrolling in a completely different position from where the cartel thought she'd be. It was still a great stroke of luck that they had found the go-fast, but the intel had narrowed it down considerably.

On board the bridge, the captain said, "Permission granted, OPS. Disabling fire authorized. Launch the small boat with a full boarding team. Oh, and get me the EO on the phone, we need those engines up and running at full speed now."

"Aye aye, sir."

The Coast Guardsman on board the helicopter, a precision marksman and trained as a sniper, ratcheted his fifty-caliber rifle, supported with compression straps, and targeted the stern of the vessel where the engine compartment was. He fired three simultaneous rounds, and the vessel immediately slowed, smoke pouring from the compartment.

In typical fashion—it was hard to tell who the biggest dope was, the humans or the drugs—the crew of the go-fast threw bales overboard and jumped over the side themselves. The thought was that if there were no drugs on board, if they had by some miracle sunk, then there was no crime. It never worked though, and the Coast Guard routinely captured thousands of pounds of drugs with street values in the multi-millions.

"Captain, the engineering officer is on the phone."

"Thank you, OPS."

"EO? It looks like we're going to have company soon, I need the engines back up to full speed so we can get back to port as quickly as possible...I don't care...Look, EO, just make it happen." Carroll slammed the phone back down on the hook, his cheeks fleetingly turning red. He took a few short breaths, calming himself before turning to Peters.

"What's the status?"

"Sir, the go-fast is still afloat, but just barely and the boarding team on the RHI has detained its crew. They've been cuffed, and PFD's have been provided. It looks like most of the packages they were trying to throw overboard are still floating. The crew is rounding up what they can and then going to meet us halfway. We should be close enough to sink the go-fast by the time the boarding team has rounded up the rest of the drugs."

"Very well, Mr. Peters. I'll be in the wardroom. Call me when we're on scene."

"Yes, sir."

"What's that?" I asked, pointing at an image on London's screen that looked like a charred rolled-up rug. We were viewing the photos he'd taken on his laptop. We were still in the parking lot and London had his laptop propped up on a large Rubbermaid container in the trunk of his SUV, the screen twisted to avoid any glare.

"We believe that's the body of a security guard. The ME is processing his dental records, as that was all that was left to identify him or her with, but we're confident the body is that of a Mr. Arnie Geller. He was last known to be investigating a silent alarm that was triggered by an access door from the parking lot to Tower Two."

I shot Carter a questioning look, and she shook her head.

"That wasn't on the news or reported to us." I inwardly cursed the feds. "We didn't know about a body. He was found here?"

London looked surprised. "Well, yes. Didn't the FBI tell you?"

I sighed and blew out my breath. "No. No, they didn't. The feds don't like sharing much with us, they like to keep everything shoved tight up their assholes."

"I thought," London said, "That you guys were feds too?" He smiled when he said it.

"We are. We're the better-looking ones, but that doesn't stop them from telling us shit if they think that gives them an edge." I shrugged. "Whatever. What do you think happened to the guard?"

London glanced at the photos on his screen and scrolled through a few more.

"Difficult to say at this point," he said. "Apart from the fact he was a crispy critter the actual cause of death will have to come from the ME. He could have had a heart attack what with the shock of the explosion, got caught in it somehow when he opened the door? Don't know."

"Okay. We'll follow up with the ME later, see what she has to say. What else do you have?"

"Not a great deal. I can tell you the media were partly right. This wasn't an accident, and it wasn't your typical fire. The arsonist used some type of accelerant. We've sent samples out to our lab for analysis."

"Could you let us know when you get the results?" Carter said. "You know, just in case our friends in black forget to tell us."

London smiled. "Sure thing." He turned to close his laptop and then said, "Oh, there is something else. Nearly forgot to tell you. We're pretty sure the fire and explosion started in the Coast Guard's prevention office. The windows in several offices blew out, but the damage seems to be concentrated in that one area.

"By the way, I wanted to express my condolences for the loss of your agents yesterday. I've lost people in the field before, it's never easy." He looked us both in the eyes, his sincerity obvious. "If there's anything I can do, please don't hesitate."

We said our thanks, left him in the parking lot and walked back to our vehicle.

Carter drove, and I said, "Well that's shitty. Another dead innocent. Bodies piling up reminds me of last year when..."

I glanced at Carter and saw her hands stiffen on the steering wheel.

"Shit. I'm sorry, Jess. I didn't mean—" I reached out to touch her shoulder, but she shrank back against the door.

"It's okay." She looked at me. "Really."

I was about to say something trite like, as long as you're sure, when I was saved from making more of an ass of myself by my phone ringing.

"Dalton," I said, answering it.

"Frank. This is Tobias, something's come up, and I need you to get back here right now, we have a visitor."

"We were heading back anyway," I looked at my watch. "We'll be back in about fifteen minutes."

He hung up without answering.

"Boss wants us back, pronto," I said to Carter.

The drive was quick, the line at the gate to access the naval base was short, and after observing the speed limit all the way to hangar forty-one, we made it to our temporary command post. You never, ever, want to speed on base. Any base. MPs take great care of their jurisdiction. Chances are that if we were speeding, they'd let us off, but if you kept doing it, they'd revoke your driving privileges. That sucked as you had to park somewhere outside of the base alongside the great unwashed and then figure out how you'd hoof the three miles to wherever it was you were going. I could do without that headache. Badges and barbecues are only good for the things they were designed for. My badge wasn't made to get me out of trouble. I'd gone through a lot of effort to get it, and I wasn't going to lose it on something stupid.

Smith was waiting for us in the conference room, and before I could ask him what was up, he said, "I'll cut to the chase. The *Glorious* was on patrol and apprehended several cartel douchebags from a go-fast. It's a bit unorthodox, but we split them up. The feebees got one, the DEA got another, and we got the third. The cutter's helo brought them in this morning. The Feds weren't happy with the idea, but word came down from DHS. They want us to compare notes later, supposed to force the fostering and sharing of information or something like that."

"Yeah, about that. They haven't been very forthcoming so far." I filled him in on what London had told us.

"Figures. Well, this could be a blessing for us then. Get our foot in the door. The Sector CO was kind enough to clear out another couple of rooms for us so we can interview the guy we have. I want you and Carter to take the lead."

"Tobias, not that I mind taking on another case, but we're pretty much two-blocked with everything we've got going on right now. How is this relevant?"

"I know you're both busy. I told you the death of our agents was your number one priority. It still is, I haven't changed my mind. With the bombings, we've been stretched thin. It's probable our agents on the beach were killed because of a drug-related incident. It seems almost too coincidental to believe that these cartel guys were just floating around with all that coke with nowhere to go. We haven't got a definitive track line yet, so don't exactly know where they were coming from, and they were doing a good job of avoiding us, but it looks as if they may have been heading for Corpus. So, maybe our beach perps were waiting for them."

He paused and looked at both of us. He looked tired. I suppose we all did, not just from working but from the stress of losing agents, relocating offices, mad men running around torching our buildings. It adds up.

Smith continued, "If we can link whoever blew up our buildings with the people who were on the beach, it could give us a break both in the case and prove it was the same group. Either way, I want you two to interview this guy and see if he'll give you anything useful. I'll see if I can get a reduction in the drug smuggling charges for this guy if he cooperates and can tell us something actionable about the death of our agents. I don't need to tell you how important that could be. If he doesn't know anything, then I'll get Special Agent Baker to take over. I want you to have first shot though."

"Sure thing, we can do that." I grabbed the case file from Smith and tucked it under my arm while I went to grab some coffee. The stuff the airedales had was way better than the sloppy muck we usually got. I'd have to make sure I didn't get too used to it. Can't afford expensive habits like posh coffee.

I game planned with Carter for a few minutes, and we looked over the case folder Smith had given us from the *Glorious*. The interview room was in the same building we were in, and no more than five minutes from talking with Smith I pulled opened the door and we marched inside. Without looking at either of the two people sitting behind the only table in the room, I slammed down the folder on the desk, channeling my inner Leroy Jethro Gibbs from *NCIS*, gently placed my coffee mug down, and looked them in the eye. That's when I noticed her cute, upturned smile and blonde hair. No, not the guy from the go-fast. The other person at the table.

I did a double take.

I recovered quickly and said, "Miss Lancaster, don't tell me you're representing this scumbag?" I gestured at the greasy specimen that was sitting next to her.

Miss Jamie Lancaster was a lawyer with Lancaster, Lancaster, and Mitchell. We'd met for the first time a few months ago when we were working on that egotistical bastard Batman Black's case. She'd been his counsel. After I got past my inherent resentment of lawyers and she'd lightened up and understood what we were doing, things got a little easier. She'd even brought me some evidence that had helped break the case. That was before Carter was kidnapped.

Anyway. It looked like she hadn't lost her touch in representing lowlifes. Her smile never faltered. Either she knew something she thought I didn't, or she thought she did.

Carter and I sat down, and we stared at the two of them across the table.

"Now don't be petulant, Agent Dalton, my client hasn't been accused of anything or even read his rights yet. If you don't behave, I will have to insist that he be released."

I thought that over for a minute while I sipped my coffee.

"And some coffee would be nice too. Could you run along, dear," she said to Carter, "and get us some?"

This time it was Carter who did a double take. She kept her cool better than I did, though.

"I'll just ring for the butler, shall I," Carter said pleasantly. "I'm sure he'll be along in a minute or two."

Lancaster's smile faltered just a wee bit.

"So," I said. "Your," I almost choked on the word, "client, was detained by the Coast Guard Cutter *Glorious* when they seized," I looked at Carter.

"Six hundred kilos," she said.

"Six hundred kilos of cocaine, with a street value of..."

"About forty million dollars," Carter said.

I raised my eyebrows, leaned back in the chair and whistled. "Man, somebody's gonna be angry. Forty million, Agent Carter. I can't imagine what'll happen to the person that lost that once they're in jail."

"Nothing good, Agent Dalton," she said.

"Miss Lancaster," I said. "I'm not really sure what it is you think you can do for your client, but it's pretty much a slam dunk as I see it."

Lancaster replied unfazed. "Perhaps it would be a tough case for the defense, but it's my client's belief that he may have something useful for you, some information."

I took my first good look at the sleazeball. It was hard to tell his height since he was seated, but he looked as if he could be about five-ten. His shoulders were blocky and his neck sinewy, supporting a head with a five-day-old beard and greasy hair. He had to be about thirty-five or so, but the years hadn't been kind to him. He was wearing a pair of USCG coveralls, still bright and shiny blue, never having been worn or washed.

"What is it he has to say?"

"Well. There are a few conditions first."

"I'm sure."

She ignored me. "First complete immunity—"

"Not going to happen," I said.

"You don't even know what he has to say yet."

"Don't care. There's no way the DA will let him walk after nabbing them red-handed with six hundred kilos. Besides being an incredibly stupid idea, the media would roast him. And you know he's up for reelection. No. What else you got?"

She paused for a moment. Whatever she had must be good, but she didn't want to give it away just yet.

"I'd like a moment to confer with my client."

I didn't move.

"In private."

I got up slowly and held the door open for Carter.

"Oh. And perhaps you could check with that butler, Agent Carter, about the coffee."

Carter didn't reply and just let the door slam behind her.

"What a fucking bitch," she seethed. "She makes me want to reach across the table and scratch her fucking eyes out."

"Now, now," I changed the subject. "What is it you think she has? Do you think it's got to do with the guys on the beach?"

She let out a breath. "Don't know. Could be. What else is that big a deal that she could ask for immunity straight off the bat?"

"I guess we'll find out soon," I said, nodding at the door as Lancaster poked her head out. We walked back in and sat down.

"My client is prepared to give you information that I believe will close out an old case of yours and perhaps shed some light on a current predicament you have."

"Predicament?" I echoed. "I'm not sure I'm fully catching your drift."

"Perhaps that wasn't the best choice of words. It doesn't matter. What my client is offering—"

"Miss Lancaster, I appreciate the bravado, and I'm sure you have your client's best interests at hand, but seriously, can we cut the shit and get down to business? I don't even know his name, where he comes from, or what the fuck he knows," I said.

She sat there for a second and studied her nails. They appeared impeccably manicured, as was the rest of her. She hadn't changed much in the last few months. If she weren't such a pain in the ass, she'd probably appear a lot prettier. Funny how personality can make a person shine sometimes, or in her case, maybe just give her a light semi-gloss glow.

"My client's name is Eduardo Davilla. He comes from a small town in the southeast of Honduras, on the border of Nicaragua. He's been holding onto a particularly juicy morsel of information, which he was saving for a rainy day, such as today. You'd never believe me if I told you what it was, so I took the liberty of contacting some of my father's old acquaintances from his law firm. They gave me enough information that corroborates, at least superficially, what Eduardo has told me. You have forty-eight hours to charge my client. I believe that will be enough time for you to check out the information I'm going to give you. If it checks out, you, your boss, the DA, even God will grant my client whatever he wants. However, all he wants is immunity to prosecution and a small thirty-six-foot sailboat."

I processed that and started to speak, but she cut me off.

"The sailboat is negotiable, of course."

"Right," I said. "Sure it is. Give me what you have, and I'll run it through the boss. I'm not promising anything, but if he agrees we'll see where it goes. But God help me, if you're wasting my time, just to get this guy a lighter sentence..." I paused. "You do know we just lost two agents, right?"

"Agent Dalton, I am truly sorry for the loss of your agents. What this man offers in return for immunity—"

"—and a sailboat."

"Quite. Well, it truly is that important. You won't be disappointed."

EIGHT

On a sweaty and slightly overcast Tuesday morning, the Monrovian flagged Long Range tanker, the Motor Vessel *Supra Reliance*, arrived in Corpus Christi. Although it was becoming increasingly common to see an empty tanker arriving in Corpus Christi, it was still unusual enough for the occasional second look, and several people in Roberts Point Park in Port Aransas snapped photos on their cell phones as the vessel steamed through the Corpus Christi Channel.

It was unusual because until recently only full tankers riding low in the water entered Corpus Christi to discharge oil products, but as this tanker was empty, much of the vessel that was typically submerged was visible.

The vessel was set to load five hundred thousand barrels of light sweet crude oil delivered via pipeline from the Permian Basin in west Texas and east New Mexico shale fields to points abroad. This particular load was being transported to South Korea, a semi-regular run.

"Captain?" The messman—a ship's term for a galley helper and sometime steward—knocked politely on Captain Roberts's open door. "The pilot on board, sir, and waiting for you on bridge."

Captain Roberts looked up from his paperwork, his glasses hanging on the end of his bulbous nose. He'd long grown accustomed to his messman's broken English. "Very well, Sandy. Please tell him I will be there momentarily."

"Yes, sir." Sandy all but bowed and shuffled backward away from the door and scurried to the bridge to inform the pilot.

In the 1970s, the US government banned the export of oil, a ban that held for over forty years. An embargo by the Arab members of the Organization of Petroleum Exporting Countries, or OPEC, had pushed the price of a barrel of oil, and consequently gasoline prices, higher and higher by restricting the amount of oil they pumped and therefore how much oil was available on the open market, massively inflating prices. To protect the country from a lack of oil due to any potential future conflict, and to build up a substantial emergency reserve, the ban on exports was enacted, except for exports to Canada. Exports to the friendly neighbor in the north were 'eh' okay.

Now, with the increased shale discoveries and new fracking technologies, and an overall surplus, the US was exporting to countries that would have usually only ever accepted OPEC oil, thus making oil cheaper worldwide, and the US ever richer.

The ship and crew would take an estimated nineteen days before they reached their destination, so they were looking forward to this port call in Corpus to grab some supplies and American products like Levi jeans and Marlboro smokes, Tennessee whiskey and Kentucky bourbon.

With the pilot on board, the *Supra Reliance* began the slow and steady transit from the anchorage into Corpus Christi proper.

The ship passed Roberts Point Park, through Corpus Christi Bay, under the Highway 181 Bridge and into Nueces Bay, where it moored up at the refinery dock. The entire channel was recently dredged to a new depth of forty-seven feet to accommodate larger vessels.

As they neared the dock, the pilot and captain stood on the port side bridge wing watching the longshoremen and dockworkers who would assist the vessel's crew tie up the tanker.

"All slow," the pilot said.

"All slow, aye," repeated the helmsman, pushing the telegraph back and forward again. The massive ship continued to slice through the water, the difference in speed imperceptible.

"All stop," the pilot said minutes later. The command echoed again by the helmsman.

Captain Roberts keyed his radio. "Chief Officer, ready lines."

The assist tugs pulled the vessel to decrease its speed while another pushed her nose into the dock.

Large lines were prepped and slung across to the facility where dockworkers manhandled them onto bollards, and the large tanker gradually eased into her berth. Soon after docking, the Coast Guard and Customs and Border Patrol officers and agents came on board to check documents, passports and for a routine safety inspection. The vessel's agent arrived along with a tech rep and an inspector for flag state, and class paperwork was completed.

Once these routine inspections were completed, the captain ordered the chief engineer, a giant of a man, to begin preparations for the oil transfer. Soon, twelve-inch diameter hoses would be connected from shore to ship and pumped from large storage tanks at the facility and into the vessel tanks. The transfer was expected to take about eighteen hours.

What Lancaster told me in the interview room threw me for a loop. She knew it would. What she said was just plausible enough to warrant checking out, so I caught the next available flight to Key West, Florida. The site of Davilla's hot tip. I hoped this wouldn't just be a wild-goose chase as I had a lot more constructive things I could be doing back in Corpus.

Key West was home of the Southernmost Point in the continental United States, Ernest Hemingway, a thriving alternative lifestyle community, palm trees, crystal clear aquamarine water, chickens, key lime pie, Fantasy Fest, roosters, tourists, mopeds, tourists on mopeds, locals on mopeds, monkeys, monkeys on mopeds—no wait, that's not right—cruise ships, and a whole shitload of sunk boats, courtesy of Irma and other hurricanes.

Before I'd left Corpus, I'd talked over the ramifications of this tip of Davilla's and what it could mean if it panned out, with Smith, and we thought it was important enough to send me down and not leave it to local LE. It wasn't that we didn't trust the fine local law enforcement establishment, more that we didn't want to look like fucking idiots if this turned ass up. We could have sent agents from the Miami office but wanted to keep this internal to our office for now. A CGIS Corpus self-preservation thing. Carter was staying back to keep working the case and to follow up with the ME, London, new Mark and so on. Or at least that's why she said she couldn't come.

I didn't think it was going to take me more than a day or so to verify Lancaster's information, but it was getting late when I arrived, and there was nothing I could do that night.

I'd flown into Miami, rented a car and driven down to Key West. It was about a three-hour drive, but it was quicker than changing planes multiple times just to try to land in Key West.

Besides, the drive down US 1—the Overseas Highway—was gorgeous. Once out of the hustle and dirt of Miami, past Key Largo, the real beauty of the middle keys became apparent. Crystal clear water, more palm trees, and a simple drive south. I opened the windows and let the salt spray and fresh air mingle with the air conditioning.

Marathon still looked a little lost after Irma. Well, in truth, a lot lost. I'd heard that the hurricane had obliterated some eleven hundred houses and sunk over two thousand boats in the state of Florida. Most of the sunk boats had been recovered—those that were impacting the mangroves, a hazard to navigation or leaking fuel. A few remained, and one of those was my target.

Right where the highway changes from two lanes to one, I got wedged in behind a wall of white. To call this white wall an RV would be an insult, and when it stopped at one of the traffic lights, I Googled the specs. I was stuck behind a futuristically designed EleMMent Palazzo Superior and, as the blurb said, 'the most luxurious mobile home in the world.' I could believe it. Forty-five feet long, thirteen feet high, coming in at a cool three million dollars. It even had an expandable roof deck.

It wasn't something I would ever buy, or could ever buy, but as the lanes finally changed to two and I wound up the peanut engine in my rental to pass, I craned my neck to see the front of this beauty. When the windshield came into view, I was stunned by the design. It looked like a futuristic spaceport. It had a wraparound windshield in an oval shape that appeared suspended about ten feet up in the air perched over the engine.

I gave a wave as I passed and kept glancing at it in my rearview mirror as it dwindled in the distance.

Arriving in Key West, I turned left at the end of US 1 and followed the road toward the airport. At Smathers Beach, I parked and took in the sunset. Reds and purples mingled with a few light clouds, the sun gradually dipped into the ocean. You could almost hear the sizzle of the seawater as the sun touched and dropped below the horizon.

I headed back to the car, drove down Duval Street, quiet this early in the evening, and checked into my hotel, right on the waterfront. I'd managed to convince the boss to give me more per diem than was normal and took full advantage of a nice hotel with a balcony.

I was only here for one night, so I didn't have much luggage and figured I'd head out for a beer along the boardwalk. I tried calling Carter on the phone, but it went straight to voicemail. I'd tried her after I'd landed as well but got the same voicemail response. She must still be working.

I found a bar that didn't look too busy and eased myself onto a stool and, after a quick look at the taps, went with a local draft beer. It seemed breweries were popping up everywhere these days. I took a swig of the beer and turned on my barstool to survey the scene. There were two women engrossed in conversation at a table nearby, sharing an appetizer of what looked like some sort of shrimp. They were dressed tropically, tight shorts, revealing tops, a slice of cleavage, length of leg, blonde hair that could have only come from a box. Two men at another table, laughing, enjoying a joke, food that was just delivered.

It was a large place, the bar running almost the length of the room. Must really hop late at night. I caught the bartender's attention and ordered fish tacos from the menu and another beer. I considered the colorful array of gins, fruit-infused vodkas, and bourbons arranged on tiered shelves behind the bar, idly wondering if I should switch my drink to something less carby, but then something in the room behind me caught my attention, reflected in the mirror behind the spirits.

A man was sitting at a corner table by himself, and he was staring at me. I studied him in the mirror through my peripheral vision, curious why somebody would be checking me out. Nobody, save for the few I worked with, knew I was coming to Key West, least of all to this bar, so it piqued my interest.

The man was in his late twenties, scruff of goatee, thin dirty blonde hair tied back in a ponytail, and he wore a light summer jacket over a loud tropical shirt, birds or flowers or something. I couldn't tell from this distance. I turned nonchalantly, beer in hand, and cast my eyes over the length of the room, not letting them alight on anyone or anything so it wouldn't look like I was looking at him. When I'd finished a circuit of the room, I looked back the same way, and when my eyes brushed over him again, he stood up and came over to the bar, sitting on the stool next to me. There were plenty of other stools.

My internal radar pinged at this unusual behavior. I wasn't yet ready to bolt or take him down, old reflexes bore hard, so I slowly turned back to the bar and placed my beer gently down on a square of napkin on the wooden bar top.

"Hey, friend," he said. "Haven't seen you here before. What brings you to town? My name's Jeff."

I nodded at him noncommittally. "Frank. Pleased to meet you. I'm just visiting."

"Visiting. Cool, cool," he said, bobbing his head. "Been to Key West before?"

"Yes."

"Man of many words," he smiled. "That's okay, I don't mind. I hope you don't think it's too forward of me, but I just love that shirt you're wearing." He reached over to touch the collar of my shirt, and I reflexively pulled back just enough so that his hand missed its mark, faltered and dropped back.

It took me a moment to register his words and accompanying actions. And then I looked in the mirror again. Two girls sharing drinks at a table, perhaps a little too close to each other. Two men at another table, heads touching, food forgotten. This single guy by himself. Me by myself. A few other random people, all wearing revealing or loud or refined outfits. And then it hit me all at once what sort of bar I'd walked into. I had thought the barman was really friendly but had put that down to being in a tourist location. No one here, however, looked like a tourist.

Sometimes I'm just a wee bit slow when I'm outside of my element.

I turned towards Jeff and put on my best sheepish grin and said, "This is a gay bar, isn't it?"

Jeff looked at me confused for a second before his expression cleared. He leaned back, clapped his hands together and laughed with joy. "You didn't know, did you? Oh, my God. I am so sorry." He leaned toward me again. "When I saw you sitting at the bar all by yourself, and you clearly looked at me in the mirror more than once, I thought that was an invitation. And let me guess, you completely missed the name of the bar, right?"

I shrugged. "The whispering willy?" Some investigator I am. "I thought it was the name of the owner or something."

He studied me for a second. "And let me guess, you're not gay, are you?"

I shrugged and then thought better of being ambiguous. "No. Sorry."

He slapped me on the shoulder, smiling. "Oh, darling, don't apologize." He got off the bar stool. "I'll leave you be."

I stopped him and said, "Jeff, it's okay, really. As long as we're straight with each other," I smiled at my pun, "I wouldn't mind the company. It's been a long couple of days." I tried a joke. "But no Mickey Finn's in my drink either."

He faked looking aghast. "Darling, Jeff never has to resort to roofies."

"I think we'll get along just fine," I said. "Can I buy you a drink? And then perhaps you could tell me a little about Key West? I heard Hemingway used to live here."

My phone buzzed in my pocket. "Excuse me for a second. It was a text from Carter.

I've been thinking, and we need to talk. I know you're busy. It can wait until you get back.

The hair on the back of my neck rose, and the fish tacos did a little dance in my stomach. Nothing good has ever come out of those four words. We need to talk.

For whatever reason, I showed Jeff the text.

"Girlfriend?" he asked.

I nodded.

"Been going out long?"

I nodded again.

"Living together?"

Once more, the nod of affirmation.

He put his hand on my shoulder again. "That's not good, Frank. I'm sorry. When do you go home?"

"Tomorrow, day after at the latest."

"My best advice is to ignore it for now. She's obviously made up her mind about whatever it is, and there's nothing you can do from here over the phone. Let it lie. See her when you get back. It won't get any worse than it already is."

I nodded again, feeling like one of those nodding donkeys on a car dashboard, the sun beating down, frying the little plastic burro brain.

"I'm sorry, Jeff," I said. "I think I should get going. If I'm still in town tomorrow, perhaps we could finish that drink. Rain check?"

"Sure thing, Frank. Take it easy."

I threw some money on the bar and walked out into the muggy night, wearily trudged the distance to the hotel, ignored the welcome of the front desk clerk, not noticing the other people in the elevator, got to my room, slipped out of my clothes and fell into bed.

The light of dawn pierced the darkness of the room through the sliver of curtains I hadn't entirely closed, and the sound of monkeys on scooters, no that's still not right, the sound of several roosters crowing brought me out of my dreamless sleep.

I went for a pee, fumbled with the in-room coffee maker, turned it to the 'crappy' setting—all in-room coffee, in all hotels, only have two settings, off and crappy—and hit the shower. This early in the morning, the pressure of the water was intense and steaming hot. I stayed there a little longer than necessary, dried off, shaved, dressed, took one sniff of my coffee before pouring it down the sink and went down to my car.

I had to drive up to Marathon, about an hour back up US 1. I could have stayed in Marathon, but really, what was the point when I was so close to Key West?

I passed several Keys, didn't see any Key deer, there's only about six hundred left, and drove over the glorious and genuinely named Seven Mile Bridge, passed Bahia Honda State Park and turned right on 15th Street.

A few old men sat around on the corner, already drinking oversized forties, resting on old milk crates in the shade of a beat-up umbrella. They ignored me as I drove past. I pulled into what used to be the 15th Street marina. The hulks of a few old, recovered vessels from Hurricane Irma sat lonesome and decrepit along the side, waiting to be shipped up north and destroyed.

I pulled up next to a work barge secured to the bulwark, with a heavy-duty sixty-five-ton American crane on board, and a small tug at the stern. The tug and barge were still here, many months after they'd been contracted to remove sunk vessels from the water, and it wasn't difficult to get them to take me out to the one that Lancaster had identified. If this was all a wild-goose chase, at least I could claim some underway time.

A guy named Jordan was in charge. He wore a red hard hat that had seen better days, work pants and a long-sleeved shirt. An unkempt beard poked out from underneath a skull bandana, giving him a surreal look in the early morning sun.

He pulled the bandana down. "Dalton?"

"That's me."

"I've looked over the plan that you guys sent down yesterday. You sure you want to go look at that area? It's a ways down Boot Key Harbor, near the end. All the vessels down there have been cleared out of the channel."

"I'm sure," I said, levering myself up onto the deck over a large tractor tire used as a fender. We shook hands. "We're looking for one boat in particular. There's a good chance it has a body on board. Someone we've been looking for. If my source is correct, it's not likely to be pretty, they've been missing for quite a while. No telling what state it's going to be in."

"We've been told. Wouldn't be the first body we've found. The divers have a decon set up in case it gets gnarly. It's not a quick process though. Have to send the divers down to scope the vessel, and then if it looks okay, we'll put slings under and gently lift the boat. Let the water drain out and hoist it on board. You have any PPE?"

"Just what I'm wearing. Should be enough for observing. The medical examiner should be along here in a minute, I don't know what he has with him."

I was wearing coveralls, composite-toed boots, and a hard-hat. Jordan had handed me a PFD. I wouldn't really be getting dirty, that was the barge guy's job.

"Alright, as soon as he's on board, we'll conduct our safety brief and cast off. If you have anything to add, safety wise or something you think the crew should know, you can say it then. Should be about a thirty to forty-minute trip under the bridge and down through the channel."

I nodded. "Sounds good."

The ME soon showed up, and we shoved off.

I have to say that the tug captain knew his shit. It looked like we were going to hit every damn thing on the way down, boats on moorings jutted out with no seeming rhyme or reason. It looked like they had just slung their hooks wherever they felt like—which they may have. A few liveaboards watched from their decks as we passed, the men bronzed and shirtless, the women bronzed and not shirt-less—which was probably a good thing—coffee in hand. A few waved. I waved back. The captain jogged and jockeyed the controls like a magician, and we were soon on scene. The spuds, giant steel poles attached to two corners of the barge in spudwells and integrated into the corners of the barge were hoisted by the crane and let loose, splashing into the water, grinding down into the mud and securing us in position.

The clear water of the Key had been stirred up by the tug's engines on our approach, and I couldn't see much through the murk. The divers suited up, the compressor began chugging to supply them with air, and one of them eased himself down a ladder and dropped from sight. I tracked his progress by the stream of bubbles coming to the surface. The depth of water down here wasn't that much, maybe eight to fifteen feet.

Time stretched. There wasn't anything I could do except watch. Nothing much was happening on deck until the divers finished their job. I slugged bottles of water from the cooler and slapped on sunscreen from a little packet I'd brought with me. An hour later, the diver radioed that he could sling the vessel, and the crane roared to life, dropping one end of a broad canvas sling. The diver had to push this underneath the vessel. One sling for the stern and one further forward. Cinching straps were tied to the slings on both sides to prevent them from slipping. This took another hour.

It was mind-numbingly dull, particularly so when all I could do was watch other people work and I couldn't see what was happening underwater. The guys on deck hustled though, and I could appreciate why they all wore long pants, long sleeves, and bandanas. The sun was brutal.

The diver radioed he was done and moved back to the barge and up the ladder. He looked exhausted and was bathed in sweat when he took his helmet off. He chugged the first three bottles of water that were handed to him in seconds.

Jordan signaled the crane operator to start winching, using hand signals, pinching his thumb and fingers together, his arm raised over his head. Slowly.

The superstructure of the vessel appeared gradually from the murk, and it looked like she was some sort of old cabin cruiser. Probably a nice ride before it sank. Water poured out of every orifice, and the cruiser slowly inched its way out of the water. When it was raised to its gunnels, the boat was maneuvered by the crane closer to the barge, and three or four six-inch hoses were thrown into the depths of the vessel, hooked up to trash pumps. As the dewatering ops began, the vessel inched its way up, supported by the crane, and in time, the name on the stern was visible. I'd half believed this was a wild goose chase, the name said otherwise.

In cheesy block letters, covered in grime and algae, the words *Reel Guts* appeared. This was one of Batman Black's personal boats. I'll be damned. Lancaster was right.

NINE

I had to wait another hour for the pumps to finish their thing before the vessel was light enough for the crane to lift it on board. There was a large hole in the port quarter, evidently what had caused it to sink, and water sluiced out with bits of boat debris, gas cans, and foam, what looked like an old shoe, pieces of random wood.

The crane slowly eased the cabin cruiser onto the deck of the barge. Once down, the crew moved in and unhooked the straps and blocked the vessel to prevent it accidentally moving.

The crew backed off and left us to it. I donned a pair of nitrile gloves and clambered over the side of the listing vessel into what would have been the cockpit. The ME was behind me, Doctor Julian Gonzalez, and I gave him a hand up.

"Freakin' reeks, doesn't it?" he said.

"Thought you'd be used to this doc," I replied.

"Death, decomposition, sure. Rotting seaweed and already cooking mollusks, not so much."

He gave me a wisp of a smile. He was a slight man, reedy thin and tall, with arms that seemed to extend from his body as if they were made of elastic. Ever watch Fantastic Four?

I shone a flashlight into the cabin. Slime oozed from the walls, and everything was covered in brown silt and grime, making even ordinary objects like the table seem surreal and out of place. I slipped a hose onto my four-gas meter and threw the end into the cabin. It took a moment for the air to pump through the hose and into the meter. I wanted to make sure there was nothing nasty in the cabin as it had been submerged for months. The meter checked for low oxygen, hydrogen sulfide present in rotting things, carbon monoxide and explosive atmospheres. I was only really concerned with a lack of oxygen or hydrogen sulfide, but the other two came free. All clear.

"Do you know where he would be?" Gonzalez asked.

"No idea. Can't be too many places he could be though. If you want to stay out here in the fresh air, I'll give you a shout if I find anything."

He nodded, and I carefully slid and slipped my way through the sloping deck of the cabin. If the smell was bad out there, it was gag-worthy inside, and I took a moment to think of fresh flowers and coffee. Didn't help. I wanted to breathe through my mouth to mask some of the smell but didn't want any of this shit in my lungs, so opted to go with the nose and bear it. I started to pull up the top of my T-shirt to cover my nose but had a better idea, and I popped my head back out. "Hey, doc. Do you have another mask?"

He reached into a pocket and rummaged around for a moment before handing over a worn-looking face mask. "It's clean, I promise. Just a bit crumpled."

"Thanks, doc. I believe you," I said in a tone of voice that said anything but. Still, I put it on and headed back inside the slime pit boat. The beam of my flashlight lit up the corners, and I made my way forward toward the bow, thinking the main berth must be that way.

Slipping on a nasty section of grime, I nearly put my foot through the floor. I tried grabbing hold of something for support, but it disintegrated in my grip. With an empty lung whoosh, I landed on my backside, creating a hell of a racket.

"You okay in there?" Gonzalez shouted.

"All good," I said, now thoroughly covered in dark green and brown sludge. Going to have to chuck these coveralls away.

Back on my feet, I gingerly made my way to the cabin door, loosely hanging on its hinges. It still took a few good tugs to open as the frame was swollen with water damage and bent out of shape. I shined my light on the oversized queen mattress, or what looked like it was once a mattress, a couple of lobsters limply hanging on, caught in the exposed springs.

The cabin itself was probably nice at one point. The remains of a mirror were on the ceiling, and the cabin was quite large, a couple of broken portholes letting in a little light. On the bed itself was a human-sized lump, decomposed, sloughed fat mixing with the grunge of the silt and algae. A couple more lobsters were nestled comfortably in the chest cavity. Remind me not to eat lobster while I was here.

"Doc. You might want to come down here."

I waited for him to slide his way through. "Oh, and mind that hole near the table," I said, almost too late. Gonzalez recovered his balance, flexible arms holding him steady.

"Here grab this," he said, as he got closer and handed me his medical bag.

He exchanged his work gloves for a pair of blue nitrile gloves. "Can you shine your light directly at the body, please Frank?"

I obliged.

Gonzalez looked over the body, gently probing. After a minute he said, "Frank, there's not an awful lot I can do in here, have to move him to the morgue."

"It's a him? How can you tell?"

"Oh, general size, shape, bone structure," he waved his hand the length of the body. "Or a very large woman." He thought for a minute. "No, definitely a male, that much I'm sure of. Not positive on the cause of death, too much muck and grime. Ditto on when he died. Can we get them to take us back to the dock, and I can get a transport here to pick up the entire vessel and take it? It'll be easier than trying to move him, or slop through all this potential evidence."

Who says ditto? "We can do that. Let's get out of here before I hurl, and we can talk on the deck."

We exited without any further drama, and I told Jordan we needed to get back. In short order, the spuds were raised, and we were chugging back up Boot Key toward 15th Street.

I called Smith while we were in transit. "Hey Tobias," I said when he answered. "I think I might need to stay here another day or two. We found a body, right where Lancaster said we would. No ID yet, except it's a male, and no cause of death...I don't know, that's why I want to stay. We're on the way back to the marina, and the ME has arranged for a transport truck back to his office. I'm going to tag along, assuming he does the autopsy today?" I looked at Gonzalez. He looked at his watch, and I could see him mentally calculating the time to unload and load. He nodded.

"Yeah, the autopsy will be done today...Okay, I'll call you when I know something. Oh, one more thing, Tobias. Have you heard from Jess? Uh huh, okay, thanks."

I mulled over what he'd said about Carter as we chugged back. I watched the wake behind us, churning up the water, and got lost in thought. The water jogged my memory to another time, many years ago, somewhere a lot colder, in Cape May, New Jersey...

It is bitterly cold, rainy and windy. A squad of Coast Guard recruits are standing at attention facing the sea. The recruits are carrying full seabags on their shoulders. The sea is rough, and waves are crashing onto the shore.

A Coast Guard company commander is standing behind the recruits. He is also at attention. His Smokey the Bear cover, chinstrap pulled taut under his chin, is dripping from the rain.

"My name is Chief Boatswain's Mate Greer. I have been in this man's Coast Guard for twenty-two years. I joined this nation's premier maritime service before most of you were born. I sailed the seven seas before you were out of diapers, most still sucking on your mama's tit. When you were in kindergarten, I was securing enemy beaches thousands of miles away. When you were in elementary school, I was chasing armed drug smugglers and interdicting aliens. When you were in middle school, I was rescuing panicking fisherman from the Bering Strait. And when you were in high school, I was being dropped from helicopters onto the decks of foreign freighters to secure them from pirates."

Chief Greer pauses and stares at the recruits. He marches slowly around the side of the recruits to the front of the formation. He stops right in the middle. Not one recruit moves, still standing at attention, eyes straight ahead. Some recruits are visibly shivering.

"You sissies may wonder why you're out here in the middle of the night. Why you're standing here in the freezing cold and pissing rain. Why you're hungry and tired and wet. Why, even when we are done here, you still have to march eight miles back to the barracks. You sissies might have back problems. Your shoulders are probably burning from carrying your sea bag. You may think that this is all bullshit. You may think of quitting. You may think of writing to your mama and telling her how hard you have it. How cold it is. How hungry you are. You know what I think?

"I think you should go ahead. You sissies should write to your mama. You should complain. You should tell how unfair it all is. And you know what you should do right after that?

"You should quit. Because I don't want you in my Coast Guard. You don't deserve to be in my Coast Guard. You haven't got what it takes to be in my Coast Guard."

Chief Greer turns and marches from one end of the formation to the other and then back to the middle again.

"This miserable night. This freezing cold night. This shit." He points to the raging ocean. "This shit, when most normal people are tucked up in bed with their hot cocoa. This shit when it's too cold to even let the damn dog out of the house. This shit when it's too windy, too wet and just too goddamned overall shitty is when we are called."

He looks along the front line of the formation, staring at each individual recruit.

"This shit is when we go. Our job is to rescue the God-fearing public when no one else can or will. Some of you may learn to drive small boats, or cutters, or helicopters or planes. But when that alarm goes off, you don't complain. You don't say you're too tired, or it's too cold, or too rough or too dangerous. You just suit up, shut up, and goddamned well go.

"If that's too much for any of you, if you don't think you can handle it, if you don't have what it takes to be a hero, then I don't want you at my back. You can go home right now.

"You can tell stories about how tough it was, or how it wasn't for you. But when you're in trouble, and you reach for that radio to call for help you can rest assured that we will goddamned well answer.

"Because that is what we do. We save people. We protect people. We are the United States Coast Guard.

"Semper Paratus.

"Recruits! Right, face! Forward, march! Left, left, left right, left…"

The banging of the barge against the bulkhead at the 15th Street marina and the roar of the tug engine brought me out of my reverie. I shivered in the heat, the memory casting a chill. Boot camp. That was one time in my life I'm glad I don't have to repeat. I shook myself and bounded ashore. I wonder what ever happened to old Chief Greer? You could always hear him coming up behind you in the barracks as his heels clicked and clacked in his shiny corfams in his slow, modulated pace. You wanted that slow click to go on past you. It was when it crept up to you and stopped just out of sight of your peripheral vision you knew you were in trouble.

"Dalton."

I jumped, expecting Chief Greer to be right behind me, but it was only Doctor Gonzalez.

"You okay?" he asked. "I've been calling your name, but you didn't answer."

I shrugged. "I'm good, doc. Just some old memories. Give me the address to your place, and I'll catch up with you. I want to go and change first."

TEN

I rolled off my coveralls as best I could and drove back down 15th Street and virtually straight across the Overseas Highway to Coast Guard Station Marathon, where I begged for a hot shower and a cup of coffee.

After I'd cleaned up and changed into spare clothes from my overnight bag, I punched the address the doc had given me into the GPS and headed north a ways to Grassy Key.

The Monroe County Medical Examiner Facility was built in the last decade, and Doctor Gonzalez took great pride in showing me around. The facility, constructed as two separate buildings connected by a breezeway—a larger one for admin, and a smaller one for autopsies—both had matching green metal roofs. The rear of the larger building had two garage doors that could be rolled up for deliveries, coroner vehicles, dead people...and the location was hard to beat. There was only one other business on Grassy Key, and tropical water surrounded the place.

The inside of the morgue was clean and efficient, with only a trace of formaldehyde and disinfectant to distinguish it. Three-wheeled stainless-steel tables, with raised edges to keep bodily fluids from oozing onto the floor, were lined up with room to work around each, and the head of the table overlapped a large stainless-steel sink, complete with various hoses to spray and wash the bodies. Large adjustable spotlights on a swing arm were secured to the ceiling, and a set of old-fashioned meat scales, also attached to the ceiling, were located nearby for weighing brains and livers and other body parts. Flat-screen monitors jutted out on steel arms from the wall for viewing X-rays and medical records. On the opposite side of the room, a giant stainless-steel reefer was recessed into the wall, four doors across by three doors high, each two feet by two feet. Behind each door was a space that could hold one body on a heavy-duty tray that slid in and out on rollers used for storing the deceased until the autopsy or investigation was concluded.

I didn't really want to be in the morgue, any morgue really. I never had much of an affinity for watching people being sliced up, but I was here now, and it was what I had to do. This particular body was bones and goop. I wasn't sure how Gonzalez would handle it, but he told me that he was going to run the autopsy in the same way he usually did, albeit with a few exceptions since the body was in a boat.

The transport truck had delivered the cabin cruiser to the back of the morgue. A small team of CSIs was going through the vessel looking for clues, evidence, the usual stuff. There was a good chance most of it had been washed away or dissolved over time. Maybe a lobster had snacked on something vital. Had to go through the motions, though, you never knew what they might find.

After they'd bagged and tagged and taken photos of every which thing, Gonzalez and his team went on board and slipped the body as best they could into a body bag, zipped it up and manhandled it out of the boat, onto a gurney, into the morgue, and onto a table.

Bag unzipped, body carefully maneuvered, more photos taken, evidence bagged, and the body sluiced down. I want to say it was washed, and the experience was typical, but when the fat and skin that was left sloughed off onto the table and into the sink, I had to be excused for a moment.

You get used to dead bodies in my line of work. Unfortunately. Or maybe it's fortunate that you get used to them, as I wouldn't be much of an agent if I couldn't stomach it. But this guy—I'd have to take the MEs word for it he was male—looked like warmed over lard. Not too warm, nothing to make it liquid, just enough to make it permeable, malleable, dripping. Warm candle wax, whale blubber.

And the smell. Imagine several fish, freshly caught, placed in a bucket, then throw in a few clams, and leave it in a car, the windows closed, parked in the hot sun for a few days. That smell, that particular smell, might come close to the reek emanating from this sloughed lard body.

What was left on the table after washing was white bleached bones poking through stringy muscles and blubber-like skin.

Doctor Gonzalez, dressed in blue scrubs, cotton facemask, surgeon's cap, nitrile gloves, and white apron, spoke into a voice-activated microphone suspended above his head on a wire. After the preliminary name, date, rank and serial number, he launched into the practical details.

"Deceased is a male, bone structure suggests a white male, severely atrophied. Wastage is consistent with submergence in a salt-water environment for a period of months. The water temperature for Boot Key Harbor where the *Reel Guts* was submerged averaged in the low seventies for the last few months."

He paused to turn behind him and sneeze. I guess it was getting to him too.

"The deceased weighs approximately sixty-five pounds and appears to be a fully grown male. Internal organs have been compromised by the effects of the water and by various crustaceans and other vertebrae feeding on the remains, what's left is basically...goop."

Gonzalez took his hands out of the chest cavity and stepped back, pulling his gloves off and his facemask down.

"I need a break. Coffee?"

I nodded, happy to get out of the room.

Gonzalez kept his scrubs on but lost the smock and poured me a cup of coffee from the pot in the break room after washing his hands.

"Thanks," I said, taking a sip. The break room was attached to the examination room and had a couch, fridge, long counter filled with a coffee pot, microwave, and cellophane-wrapped popcorn packages. A wide window showed the beautiful weather outside, juxtaposing the almost frigid air conditioning.

"So," I said, "is goop a professional medical term?"

"I don't usually take breaks mid autopsy," he started.

"It's okay, doc. I get it."

He looked at me quizzically, with a slight turning of the head like a dog that wants to understand but isn't quite there. After a moment he continued. "No, I don't think you do. I haven't been a medical examiner for many years. I've only recently taken the position of Chief ME here since my predecessor retired suddenly last month." He scratched his head. "I'm used to more of a clerical role," he attempted a brief smile. "I'm sure they'll get someone to take over soon enough, but funding..." he trailed off.

"No worries. It gives us a chance to talk." It was odd seeing him so open. I didn't know the guy, and he could have said any reason for needing a break, and I'd be none the wiser. It made him somehow more human, more endearing. I liked the guy for his honesty, a rarity in my field. "Do you have any clues about identity or cause of death yet?"

Gonzalez poured himself some more coffee and then waved the pot at me. I shook my head. "Not entirely. Fingerprints are of no use, as he doesn't have any good flesh left, same for the eyes. I haven't had a chance to look at his teeth yet, but if we can get an imprint, it shouldn't take long to get those results back. Dental records are uploaded by every dentist in the country, a bit like fingerprints are in CODIS." He sat down on the couch, crossing his legs, and looked out the window for a moment. "As to cause of death, I'm going to have to remove the little remaining flesh that's left on him. There's nothing detectable in what's left on the outside, so hopefully, they'll be something underneath.

"The time of death is a little harder. I've done some research on this, so can give you a ballpark figure if that'll help. Of course, my final report will have more accuracy."

I nodded. "Sure. Whatever you've got."

Gonzalez stood up suddenly and paced slowly in the room. "Submerged bodies are tough to pigeonhole. We do know that they decompose slower in water than on land. Warm water, however, speeds up the process understandably faster than cool water. Salt water also speeds up the process considerably over brackish or fresh water. Saponification has already occurred and is almost complete." He turned to me and saw my blank stare, frowning slightly, remembering I wasn't a lecture student. "Saponification, that's when the skin peels. The waxy, white hue we saw on some of the skin that's left is the next stage—"

"The lard look?"

"Quite. All the hair falls off the body, most of the internal organs putrefy, but the heart seems to stay the longest. We can guess, not really the time of death, but the month of death, by the stage of putrefaction, knowing the average water temp, salinity and so on. But it really is a ballpark figure, you understand."

I nodded again. The doc was good at explaining, and he moved his flexible arms around in an expressive manner, never spilling a drop of coffee.

"The only thing we don't know is the amount of damage caused by lobsters, crabs, shrimp, and the like. My best guess is about two months, give or take a month. Like I said, I hope to identify him by his dental records, and maybe when he's completely cleaned up, I can see if there's an obvious cause of death. If it was something like a heart attack, drowning—intentional or otherwise—or some other natural causes we won't know. His lungs are gone, his heart has been eaten, well, you saw him."

"Okay, thanks, doc. If it's okay with you, I'm going to skip the rest of it and head back to Texas. I don't think there's a lot more I can do here. How long 'till the CSI techs finish cataloging the evidence and you get a match on his dental."

"I've instructed the techs to keep working. The *Reel Guts* has been processed, and they're drying things out, seeing if any papers on board are recoverable. I've taken the liberty of sending the GPS and nav gear to your man at the Domex office in Corpus. He told me to keep everything submerged in seawater and ship it as is. The techs are on that too. As to dental records," he shrugged. "It could be as soon as a matter of hours. If I don't get a hit though, I can try extracting his DNA from his bone marrow and running that, but not everyone has their DNA recorded so it might be a long shot."

We shook hands, and I headed out to the car, the blast of heat hitting me as soon as I opened the door. I was sweating before I even got the car started. I missed my truck with its remote start.

ELEVEN

It was raining the morning after I got back to Corpus. It seemed fitting for the occasion. Although I was a CGIS agent and wore civvies all the time, I was still an active duty Coastie. Accordingly, today, for the funerals of Miner and Browning, our deceased CGIS agents, I was wearing my Service Dress Alphas, a blue jacket with rank and ribbons, a white shirt, blue tie, white gloves, and shiny synthetic corfam shoes. The Coast Guard dress uniform. The rain pattered on my combination cover, slid along the top and dripped silently onto my shoulders. It was a trivial discomfort to endure.

I was standing at attention, along with Smith, Carter, a handful of other agents who could be pulled from investigations, and the Coast Guard contingent from the Sector. The Corpus Christi Police and Fire Departments, Maria Romero, the mayor of Corpus Christi, and many, many others also attended to pay their respects. Several rows of chairs held grieving relatives dressed in shades of black, leaning on each other's shoulders, bleary-eyed and sad. In all, perhaps there were as many as two hundred of us gathered silently in the rain at the Coastal Bend State Veterans Cemetery. It was a solemn place, as it was supposed to be, only opened in the last few years, and they had done an excellent job as the final resting place for those who served their country.

I could see the caskets of Browning and Miner, shrouded in the flag of the United States of America. Just beyond, the Coast Guard Honor Guard was standing at attention.

A chief petty officer I hadn't seen before marched slowly toward the honor guard. When he was behind the seven-man team, he quietly called out orders.

"Honor guard, attention!" They were already at attention, but if it was possible, they stiffened even more.

"Standby. Ready. Aim."

The seven-man team simultaneously raised their rifles to their shoulders and pointed them skyward.

"Fire."

The discharge of the rifles rolled across the cemetery, and a cloud of gunpowder heavy with the smell of cordite floated in the damp air. Birds took off cawing raucously, startled by the significant concussion.

"Ready. Aim. Fire."

Another salvo rocked the veteran's cemetery. And then the last command was barked, "Ready. Aim. Fire."

Twenty-one shots in all.

"Honor Guard. Present arms!"

The bugler began his soulful playing of TAPS. Everyone in uniform saluted slowly. A slow salute is a sign of respect at funerals, and TAPS had never felt like such a lonely song.

A sounding of the final retreat, lights out, and the final, ultimate end.

These were good men who shouldn't have had to die.

As the bugler wound down, the last note long and sonorous, the hand salute was dropped, arms gradually lowered in unison.

As there were two caskets, two different sets of honor guard members folded the flags simultaneously. It was deliberate, slow, and done with the utmost of reverence. Once both flags were folded in the traditional triangular shape, salutes once more flawlessly executed, one of the honor guard took the flag in his arms, folded to his chest and marched slowly to Browning's widow.

He kneeled in front of her and presented her with the flag, saying, "On behalf of the President of the United States, the Commandant of the Coast Guard, and a grateful nation, please accept this flag as a symbol of our appreciation for your loved one's service to country and the Coast Guard." Standing, he slow saluted her, did an about-face and returned to the casket.

Tears streamed down her face, and she hugged her three kids, all weeping. We watched in silence as the other flag bearer approached Miner's widow and did the same thing.

I needed a drink, a smoke, and to catch those bastards. Not necessarily in that order.

Tobias Smith held the wake at his house. He lived in the Southside area of Corpus, south of Yorktown Drive, about as close as you could get to nature without swampland overrunning the place. I'd been to his house before—a bulky brick two-story, an in-and-out circular driveway, and an imposing mahogany front door, which was open. The waft of cooled air hit my damp uniform, giving me a chill.

I took my jacket off and loosened my tie, throwing the jacket over a chair in the dining room. I didn't see anyone I knew, so walked through the kitchen to the backyard.

Tobias had an impressive in-ground pool. It looked like it was about thirty feet long with a pergola to one side offering shade, and an integrated hot tub at the other, the water flowing into the pool in a small waterfall. I grabbed a burger from the grill, spied Smith, and headed for the shade. The sun had come out, brutal after the rain, and my shirt clung to me, starting to steam a little.

"How you doing?" Smith said as he approached.

I nodded at him, sat and said, "About as well as can be expected I s'pose. But better than his folks, I guess."

Miner and Browning's widows were huddled together on the other side of the pool near the hot tub. Some kids were splashing around in the pool; I couldn't tell if they were theirs or some others. Life goes on.

My cell vibrated in my pocket, breaking my reverie and any respite for good-intentioned platitudes.

"Dalton," I said, around a mouthful of burger. The fat squirted out and dribbled onto my white dress shirt.

"Shit."

"Agent Dalton? This is Aidan. I—"

"Sorry, who is this?" I glanced at the phone, but I didn't know the number.

"Aidan. In the Domex lab, I have some—"

"Right, sorry, Aidan, couldn't place the name for a second." New Mark.

"That's alright, agent. Listen, I know you're probably at the wake, but we've had a breakthrough with the evidence that the ME in Florida sent over. I think you need to come down here and take a look."

"This can't wait?" I said, trying to wipe the fat off my shirt and only succeeding in making it smear more. "And where is here anyway? I thought the lab was destroyed in the fire?"

"It was. Well, the lab was, not the equipment. The new Sector building by the airport was already finished, we just accelerated the move in schedule somewhat, we'd already moved all the machines. I think we're the only ones here for the moment. Anyway, I think you need to come down here right now, it's not something I can talk about over the phone, I need to show you. You, ah, won't be sorry, I can assure you."

I stood up, took another bite of burger, and threw the rest in the trash. "I'll be there in twenty."

I walked over to the bereaved, said my condolences, and headed for the house. Smith caught me as I was putting my jacket back on.

"You leaving already, Frank?"

"Yeah. Aidan thinks he has some information I need."

"Aidan?"

"New Mark, Domex guy."

"Ah. Right. Keep me posted. Are you taking Carter? Where is she?"

"Don't know. I don't need her for this, I'll call her if I do."

He grabbed my arm to stop me. "Everything okay between you two?"

"Peachy, Tobias. Just peachy." I gave him a weak smile, shook off his arm, left the house, got in my truck and headed for South Padre Island Drive and the Corpus Christi International Airport.

The new Sector building had come about because the Coast Guard, mostly the airedales—what non-flight crew guys call the flight crew guys—needed a place with a longer runway. The old Falcon jets were being phased out, and the new HC-135 Casa prop planes weren't as nimble. The Navy had refused to let the Coast Guard move to a building nearer the current runway at the Naval Air Station, so we'd given them the middle finger and upped and moved to a brand-new custom building by the airport, along with everyone from the downtown building.

We hadn't actually moved yet, but the fire had spurred everyone's desire to get into gear, and by the end of the month I expected the whole place to be operational.

I parked outside the building, the black tarmac radiating heat like a motherfucker. I walked quickly, half expecting my patent leather corfams to melt, and I'd be left walking in hot plastic goo.

They'd done an excellent job with the entrance. It was expansive, a long, cool corridor filled with photos of the Sector and Air Station throughout history.

I called Aidan on my cell. "Hey, this is Dalton. I'm in the main lobby, where you at?"

"I'll be right out."

He was. I followed him down a corridor that wasn't quite finished yet, either that or battleship gray was the color they were going with. I shook my head. A multi-million dollar building and this was the best color scheme we had?

The lab looked like the old one, probably on purpose. Large screens hung from the ceiling, and various machines the old Mark had told me about, but could only guess at now, rested on countertops. Everything gleamed and shone, looking like a set straight out of CSI or NCIS.

Aidan swiped at a screen, and an image of the Gulf of Mexico appeared. "We managed to download the data from the GPS unit that the ME in Florida forwarded us from the tech guys. He followed my directions and kept everything submerged in salt water, and it was a snap to dry it out and get it going."

"What did you get?"

Aidan was a tall man, strong and broad in the shoulders, and his short-sleeved shirt showed the definition in his arms. A shock of unruly brown hair framed his face, and his spectacles perched on the end of his nose gave him a professorial look. He'd told me at some point when he joined our team that he rock climbed for a hobby. Judging by the way he filled out his shirt, it looked more than a hobby to me.

Aidan swiped across the screen again, and a dotted yellow line appeared from one side of the Gulf to the other.

"Obviously, the endpoint is where you discovered the sunk vessel, but if we zoom in here," he waved his hands again, and a close-up image popped up, "you can see the start point." He stood back and beamed, pleased with himself.

I took a step closer to the screen, almost touching it, but remembering the old Mark's admonishment like the breath of a ghost in my ear.

I dropped my hand. "This is Aransas Pass."

"Yes."

"Just up the street."

"Yes, again."

I studied it for a second longer. "It makes sense I suppose, it was one of Black's boats. Did you get anything else? I mean, this is interesting an' all, but I don't see anything earth-shattering."

Aidan tried to hide the smile by covering his mouth and coughing.

"Out with it," I said.

He coughed for real this time. "I was trying to build the suspense."

"I have quite enough of that already," a little ice in my voice, "spit it out."

"Okay. Sorry. Poor timing. The results from the ID of the deceased came back."

I made a rolling motion with my hand. "And? Don't make me wring your neck for the information, Aidan, this is getting tiresome."

He held his hands up in supplication. "Okay, okay. The ME couldn't find dental records that matched the deceased. Apparently, the guy had some recent work done, enough so that it changed the structure of his jaw."

"Wouldn't that have still shown up on records?"

"I thought the same thing, but the ME said that if you had enough money, you could always find dentists and doctors willing to perform surgery for some under the table transactions."

I nodded. "Go on."

"So, he extracted the dead guy's DNA. That doesn't always work as it would have to have been recorded somewhere, but the ME got a hit."

I urged him forward with my hands again. It was like pulling teeth with this guy.

"I believe you know him." He waved his hands at the screen again, and an image appeared that I thought I'd never see again in a million years.

I sucked in a breath. "Fuck. That's Lewis, the old SAC."

"Yes, it is. And an associate of the infamous Batman Black."

"Yeah." I stared at the fucker on the screen, and his stupid smiling eyes contradicted the guilt that he must have hidden. Lewis used to oversee this CGIS office as the Special Agent in Charge. He'd been taking bribes from Black for decades, ever since he was a junior officer. He'd fled when we'd busted Black, and no one knew where he'd gone. We'd put out BOLOs, flagged his passport, alerted TSA and Border Patrol, but he never showed up. Now I know why.

"Any idea how he died?"

"The ME's still working on that. He's contacted our own ME, Doctor Hutchins, and they're collaborating on some of the more technical issues. Seems our doc is a renowned expert in the field of submerged and recovered bodies. They hoped to have something soon, but the body was in a pretty bad shape from what I hear. Well, you saw it, you know."

I nodded. "You heard right." It wasn't an image that I wanted to remember, and now that I could put an actual face, Lewis's, onto the body, made it seem even more real.

I was about to leave, but Aidan stopped me.

"I saved the best for last. The CSI techs in Florida sent over whatever they found from the vessel. Most of it is trash, papers, and documents that we couldn't hope to get a read on, being submerged for so long, but we did recover a thumb drive. Again, it was submerged in water, so we had to dry it out slowly. A lot of the data was corrupted, and I'm still working on that, pushing it through various algorithms to try and clean it up, but on one file we found a name. Eduardo Davilla."

"Shit," my heart started pounding a little harder in my chest. "That's the name of the cartel guy we've got. You mean to tell me that Lewis was involved with the cartels as well as Black?"

Aidan shrugged. "I don't know. It seems likely. They have many, many ways of getting people in and out of the country. Lewis could have contacted them for an escape route."

"Doesn't explain why they would have killed him, though."

"No, it doesn't, maybe they didn't. Hopefully, the ME can identify the cause of death."

I looped back to where we were holding Davilla. Luckily it was offsite from Tower Two, so it hadn't been compromised. I called Carter along the way to meet me there. We had to wait for Lancaster to show up.

"So, Eduardo," I said, sitting down at a metal table in the interview room. Carter sat next to me, Davilla and Lancaster were already seated across from us. "That lead you gave us, much to my surprise, it did give us some interesting information. Now that we know who was on that boat care to enlighten us on how you know?" Carter had changed out of her uniform. I was still wearing my dress pants, but after some rummaging around I'd managed to find a reasonably clean gym shirt to replace my burger juice soiled uniform shirt.

"Agent Dalton," Lancaster said, placing a hand on Davilla's arm and briefly shaking her head. "My client will not answer any of your questions until he is offered and accepts immunity from all prosecution. That was the deal we put on the table in exchange for information that led you to identifying SAC Lewis," she paused for a moment, adding, "and don't forget the sailboat."

"Right, let's not forget that nugget," I said. They'd added a wall clock for décor since we'd last been in here, and the second hand ticked ominously.

I nodded to Carter, and she placed a folder on the table between us.

She tapped the folder and said, "This contains the immunity agreement. The DA was hesitant to sign it, but our ASAC, Smith, persuaded him it was in the best interests of the United States. I hope Eduardo, here," she stared at him, "can follow through with his end."

Lancaster picked up the folder and scanned through the file. Carter had put handy little 'sign here' stickers in the appropriate places. Cute.

"Eduardo," Lancaster said, "the immunity agreement seems to be valid. I would advise you as your legal counsel to ask any questions you have now, before signing."

"Of course," I said, "if you don't sign, we'll just prosecute you for running drugs. That's life in prison with no chance of parole."

"Don't threaten my client, Agent Dalton. You know better than that. Anything signed under coercion is inadmissible."

"It wasn't a threat, Miss Lancaster. It was the truth. I'm investigating the deaths of two federal agents, and I don't have time to play games. What's it going to be Eduardo?"

He glanced at the documents, seeming almost disinterested. "I need a new identity as well. The cartel will kill me if they know I've given you anything." His English was impeccable, not what I had expected.

Carter nodded. "We've set up for the US Marshal's to provide you with new IDs, and a place to live, somewhere mutually agreeable, rent paid for six months. You'll have to get a job of course, and we've given you a social security card and basic background cover. I assume you can do something besides smuggling drugs?" She smiled sardonically.

He shrugged. "I used to be a mechanic. I can manage."

"There is one caveat," I said, and Eduardo raised an eyebrow. "If you break the law, so much as get a jaywalking ticket, then the deal is off, your cover will be blown, and we'll let the cartel know where to find you. If you try to run or leave the country, the same applies. We'll give you immunity, but you must become a model citizen from here on out. Any deviation and the deal's off."

Eduardo looked at Lancaster. For once, she didn't say anything, just shrugged.

"I'll sign," he said, and scribbled in the marked spaces, pushing the folder back to Carter. She glanced through it to confirm he'd signed and nodded to me that it was good.

"So," I said, spreading my arms wide. "Tell me what Lewis was up to, why your name was on an encrypted thumb drive, and how he died."

He gave us what we had mostly figured out. The cartel was offering Lewis transport out of the country. He'd holed up in Florida to await the final details, but when—Eduardo wouldn't say who—arrived to smuggle him out, he didn't show.

He shrugged. "The contact waited for a few hours, much more than was necessary, but Lewis had paid us well, so he gave him extra time. When he didn't show, it was no loss to us. We had the money. We didn't ask questions. He knew the deal."

"So you have no idea how he died?"

"None. Like I said, no concern of ours. As far as we cared, it was a win-win deal. We had the cash and didn't have to do any work."

I leaned forward. Eduardo didn't flinch. "Are you sure you didn't just kill him? Save you the hassle of smuggling him?"

"Believe what you want agent. It doesn't matter to me."

"How were you going to get him out?"

"That's not something I can tell you. We have various networks. I'd only be guessing." He shrugged again. Eduardo was a master of the noncommittal shrug.

"You're not giving me much to go on here, Eduardo. We found Lewis like you said, but you can't confirm or deny how he died, you won't tell me how you were going to get him out, I'm beginning to think we may have to rethink this whole immunity deal. I can't go back to the DA and tell him we got nothing."

"Agent Dalton, why don't you give my client and I a few minutes?" Lancaster said in a sweet tone.

"Sure. Think about what I said, Eduardo."

Outside the room, we went on the hunt for some airedale coffee. It felt like a month ago I'd last been here.

"What do you think?" Carter said.

"I don't know." I took a swig of coffee. It was good. I waved the mug at her. "You should try some."

She shook her head.

"We never would have been able to close the loop with Lewis if he hadn't told us where to look, but he hasn't given us much else. Lewis could have stayed lost, and we still wouldn't be any better off than we are now."

"So it's a bust." A statement, not a question.

"Maybe. Depends on what Lancaster's talking to him about. She knows it's not enough for us to follow through with the immunity."

"But he signed it."

"I didn't see him sign, beats me where the paperwork could have gone," I said, shrugging.

Carter frowned. "That's not right, Frank. He did sign it, you and I both witnessed that." She paused for a beat. "I'm so clumsy though, I think I might have accidentally shredded it."

I smiled and rubbed her shoulder. "Come on. We've given them enough time."

Back in the room, there seemed to be a shift in attitudes. Lancaster was looking a little more comfortable, but Eduardo looked lost. A single bead of sweat rolled down his forehead.

Carter and I sat down and waited. He who talks first loses. An old used-car salesman trick. Eduardo folded first, and I had him.

"You realize that if I tell you this, my life is over," he said.

"If you don't tell us, your life will be spent rotting in prison," I said.

Eduardo looked at the ceiling as if beseeching help from some higher power. As far as I knew, the only higher power directly above us was the Sector commander's office, and I doubted he'd be helping Eduardo much.

"A drink of water, perhaps?" he said.

"Later. Stop stalling, or we walk out, and the immunity goes with us."

He leaned back in his chair, defeated. "Fine. I get it. You want something that you don't know, something that will help you? Something that will guarantee my immunity?"

I nodded. "That's about the size of it."

"Fuck. I hope you realize the importance of what I'm about to say." He looked around the room once more, as if he was half expecting to be busted out by armed cartel operatives. Nothing happened. This wasn't the movies. "A few days ago, perhaps. There was a delivery by a fishing boat to the Gulf Coast here. The boat was a cartel boat, but the shipment wasn't drugs, it was men."

That got my attention. I glanced at Carter, she'd perked up too. Lancaster remained silent, no doubt already privy to the details.

"The men swam ashore and landed on the Padre Island Sea Shore," he continued. "I believe your men may have encountered them."

I leaned back in my chair. This is what I really wanted. I tried to calm my breathing.

"How did they get here undetected? We have patrols, cutters, airplanes. How did we miss them?"

Davilla leaned back and blew out a breath. "I'd like that water now, please."

"Later. Tell us how they got here. Who are they and how many of them are there? Don't fuck around with this, Eduardo."

A fleeting smile. "Four men. Apparently, they didn't speak much to the fishermen. I wasn't there, but that is what was passed. Even so, the fishermen on the boat thought they were most likely Americans."

Four of them. Confirmation. "Why'd they think that?"

He shrugged. "Hair, skin tone, mannerisms. Fishermen are good judges of character, seeing all types."

Thinking of Black, who owned a fishing fleet before he died, I let that slide. "How did they get in undetected? What's their plan?"

Davilla looked pained. "I can tell you the first. I have no idea what their plan is though."

I nodded. "Go on."

"It's simple. You already know we have informants," he said.

"Like Lewis, sure."

Davilla smirked. "Yeah, like him. And before you ask, I have no idea about any others. But, besides that, we use a lot of social media. You'd be amazed at how easy it is to figure out your ship movements, your patrols, when one of your planes are broken." He paused for a breath. "I could really do with that water."

"In a minute," I said. "Keep going."

He shrugged again. "Alright. Take some guy who's stationed on one of your cutters. Let's call him Jimmy. He's coming off duty, invites two of his buddies from the crew out for a few beers after work, and they stop by their local on the way home. Jimmy takes a selfie and posts it on Instagram, his settings automatically 'checking' him into the bar."

Carter interrupted. "I get where you're going, but we've all been well trained to keep our data private and to not accept random friend requests. So your social media trawling can't be that extensive."

Davilla shrugged again. "Maybe," he said. "Maybe not. See Jimmy, has a new friend. Let's call her Sofia. Jimmy knows enough to not accept random friend requests. He's done his due diligence before he accepted Sofia's follower request, and having looked at her profile, she seemed legit. Jimmy wasn't convinced he did know her, but he met so many people, he might have. Besides, Sofia's profile picture is hot, so naturally, he clicked accept and now had a new follower whom he hoped he would see around.

"But check this out," Davilla continued. "What Jimmy doesn't know is that his hot new friend's name isn't Sofia, but Jose. And Jose is an overweight, sweaty dude who wears grease-stained tank tops. Jose was also an accomplished hacker who worked for the Sinaloa cartel, posing as a female redhead one day, a voluptuous female blonde another, a guy who looked like The Rock another—whatever, you get the idea."

"Okay," I said. "So, you've got this cartel guy posing as a hot girl, who befriends a Coastie on social media. How does that help. He's not likely to post his patrol schedule."

"Doesn't have to. Jose knows through looking at Jimmy's posts that he works on a Coast Guard cutter. And if Jimmy is in a bar with his friends, it's a safe bet he isn't getting underway for a patrol. Now, multiply that by another guy that works at an air station, a woman who works at a search and rescue station and so on, you can piece together a pretty good snapshot of what's going on."

I took a moment to process that information. "That's insane." I stared at him. He didn't blink or flinch. I think he was telling the truth.

"Okay. Say we believe you," Carter said. "Where did these guys come from. These Americans?"

"Again, I don't know that. We were paid a great deal of money through various deals and cash transactions. Most times middlemen are used to protect the identities of the parties involved. It isn't our job to ask questions, we don't ask why. I know if they were coming here, it wasn't to play pat-a-cake, it was to fuck up some shit. That much seems obvious."

I sat there in silence for a moment, waiting for more, but nothing came. At least that confirmed Doctor Hutchins' theory of four men. Eduardo looked spent, as if this information had drained him like a stuck pig. If there were four men, and Miner and Browning had shot two, that left two. Two fuckers in the US up to who knew what the fuck. Knowing this, it seemed obvious they must have set the building on fire, but what next?

TWELVE

"What have you got for me, doc?" I asked as I entered the morgue. We were lucky that the morgue was located away from Tower Two. "Frank, Jessica. Any news? Did you catch the scum that killed—" her throat hitched, and she didn't continue, turning away and grabbing a tissue from the cuff of her lab coat, wiping her eyes. "I'm sorry," she said. "I don't..."

"It's okay, doc," I said softly. I gave her some space. "We haven't caught them yet, but we will. We've just got confirmation on how many of the fuckers there are or were."

"How many?"

"You were right. There were four of them. Our boys did good, got the other two," I changed topics. "I have to say that was great work with the DNA testing. I heard you were an expert in submersed bodies? I don't suppose you know how Lewis died do you?"

Hutchins smiled tightly, her mouth creasing in the corners, a sort of anti-smile. "I'm glad we know what happened to the fucker. Excuse my French, but he was." She smiled a bit brighter. "As for cause of death, I'm sorry to say that it's going to be noted on the death certificate as inconclusive. There didn't seem to be any obvious signs of trauma beyond normal atrophy, no bullet holes or caved in skull. No smoking gun, as it were." She shrugged. "It could have been something as simple as carbon monoxide poisoning, but without a good blood sample to test for carboxyhemoglobin, there's no way to know for sure. If I had to guess it would be that or drowning, but his lungs were gone, so like I said, inconclusive."

I mulled that over and looked at Carter. She shrugged. "I guess it doesn't much matter in the end," I said. I scratched the back of my head. "Anything you can tell me about the two people we're chasing?"

"I'm sorry, Frank. I wish I had something. I'll keep working on it, and I'll text you the minute I know," she said and tucked the tissue she'd dabbed her eyes with back into the sleeve of her lab coat.

We left the building and walked back to the truck. I was unsure of our next step. The hair on the back of my neck was telling me something bad was coming. Since they'd destroyed our office, it seemed likely they might still be in town, but I didn't know for sure.

I put the truck in drive. "Want something to eat?"

Carter shrugged. "Sure."

I had the feeling that although we had closure on Lewis, it had dredged back all the bad memories of her kidnapping, as she was unusually reticent in the morgue.

The cruise ship *Nexus Joy* was operating beautifully, and exceeding the expectations of the captain, Leif Gunnarsson. He sat in his bridge chair, a heaving monstrosity of leather and chrome, taking in the sunrise through the tinted bridge windows. The dull hum of machinery and the crackle of radio traffic were the only noises.

Gunnarsson was a morning person by nature and watching the sunrise while on board a ship was one of his favorite pastimes. While at sea, it was rare indeed that he would miss a sunrise and could recall only a handful of times that he had.

"Mr. Jurgen. What is our ETA to Corpus Christi?"

"Captain, we should be in range of the pilot boat by 0500 tomorrow. The weather forecast is clear, and it's a straight shot up the coast from Costa Maya. I don't anticipate any problems."

"Very well. I'll be taking breakfast in my stateroom. Inform me if anything comes up."

"Yes, sir."

Gunnarsson raised his bulk from the chair and left the bridge, heading one deck down to his stateroom where he dialed the stewards.

James King blew out a frustrated breath and sat back on his knees. "Oh come on, you know you want to," he said, adding, "Please?"

"And you know begging really turns me on, right?"

King was sitting at the feet of his wife, Amaya Dabiri, and he was seriously beyond blue-balled.

"Ami, I wasn't begging," King said in what he hoped was a neutral tone. "I was just asking why we couldn't."

"Couldn't what?" she said.

"Come on, you know, the thing."

"You're pathetic, James. You can't even say it. You say you want it so bad, and even in here," she waved her arms around their small living room, "in the privacy of our own home, you can't even pluck up the courage to tell me what it is you want."

King sat on the plush rug, a present from his father-in-law, and ran his hands through the luxuriant weave. He fought to stop going red, tried to control his breathing, and finally gave up. Standing, he said, "I've had enough of this shit, Amaya. You always put me down. What the fuck is it you want? I just don't know anymore. I'm not sure I know you anymore either."

"I want you to be a man, James. A man like the one I married, a man that sticks up for himself, a man that's not afraid to speak his mind, tell me what he wants, demands it of me as every husband has the right to demand it of his wife."

"This is stupid," he said, turning.

"And that is why you'll never have me. Running away like a little boy. Run, James, run. Go cry like a baby. A man would stand his ground. A man would take control." Amaya knew just what to say to King to draw him back.

King clenched his fists, breathing hard, trying to regain control of his emotions. "Enough," he said. "You will stop this right now. Take your clothes off. I want you on your hands and knees."

"Make me, James."

King stood over her, pulled her up from the couch, grabbed her shoulders. He snaked his hand to the top of her back and with a harsh tug pulled down the zipper of Amaya's dress, sending it to the floor. Underneath her dress, she wore white lace panties, stark against the brown of her skin. Her breasts pushed at the delicate bra she was wearing.

"Is this what you want?" King said.

"Yes, James. Take charge. Be the man."

"Like this?" He fumbled with her bra, the clasp coming loose and her ample breasts brushed against his chest.

"This is what you want?" he repeated.

Amaya nodded.

"Bend over then."

"Such a way with words, James. You make me so wet." He didn't catch the sarcasm.

King loosened his belt, and his pants slid to the ground. He yanked his boxers down, his erection immediate. He turned Amaya around and pushed her head down, so she was bent over, her brown ass wiggling in the air, and grabbed her hips. When Amaya felt the first probing touch of his erection, she straightened up, turned and grabbed him, locking eyes.

"Not so fast, James," she said, her voice low and husky. A voice well versed in manipulation. She played with him, nibbled his ear and whispered, "I need you to do a little something for me first."

She turned him back to the couch, touching him, rubbing him, pushing him down, kneeling in front of him. "I love it when you act like a man."

"Wasn't acting," said King, almost sulking.

"No, of course not, James. What I meant was I love it when you take charge. It turns me on," she continued in the same manipulative voice, King oblivious to anything but her touch. "And I want to have sex with you, James, I do. It can be like the old days, do you remember the old days James, when we first met?"

King closed his eyes, and Amaya knew he was remembering their first months together. She continued to stroke him. "Don't you remember, James. How wonderful it was?"

He groaned, and Amaya knew she had total control of her husband. She despised the little feckless shit. "Now before you have your way with me, my man, my strong man, I just need you to do a little favor for me at work tomorrow. It shouldn't take long." Amaya continued to work his penis with her hand, lowering her head.

"Oh God, anything. Just don't stop."

"If I do this for you, James," she said, locking eyes with him, "you have to promise you'll do this little favor for me, and then when that's done, we can do what you want."

"Yes. Anything you want, Ami."

"Good. Tomorrow, James," she said, sliding her tongue along his shaft. "I want you to go to work and, mmmm, you taste good. I want you to add two crew names to the *Supra Reliance* roster."

"What?" King said, momentarily breaking from his ecstasy. "What do you mean? I can't do that, I'll lose my job, it's just not...ahhhh."

"What was that, James?" She stroked him harder. "I thought you said you'd do anything for me? All I need you to do is log on, add two names, log off, come home to me, and we can fuck like animals."

She gave him an extra hard jerk, finishing him, and wiped her hands on his shirt.

"Tomorrow, James. And then we can do anything and everything you want, you can have all of me. Any way you want." She kissed him on the mouth, purposely rubbing her breasts in his face when she stood, lingering a little longer than necessary, and then walked away, King's eyes lingering on her sashaying behind.

King sat on the couch, entirely spent. Amaya, his Amaya, was like a drug he could never get enough of. His mind was in a whirl with what they would do tomorrow. He was entirely under her control. He would do it. Anything she asked. He added and deleted names to rosters and manifests all the time, so who cared about these two if he could have Amaya?

The next morning, James King drove to work, intending only to be there long enough to log on and complete what Amaya wanted. He was positively vibrating with unfulfilled sexual energy and felt he could probably power a small city if he were hooked up to the grid.

Amaya had stoked his fires again this morning, reminding him what was waiting for him when he came home, spurring him on.

It hadn't always been like this, this manipulation. Their marriage had been one of joy and wonder to begin with, and it was only after they moved back home to America—well, back home for James; Amaya had never lived in America—that the trouble started.

King had met Amaya a few years before, while he was overseas in Rotterdam, in the Netherlands. King was a shipping agent and regularly traveled the globe, ensuring the large freight vessels that pulled into port had crew relief, medical supplies, engine spare parts—anything they needed to keep the crew moderately happy and the vessel running. He arranged flights for the crew to go home after their contract was complete, cleared shipping documents, manifests, and passports with customs and immigration, liaised with the coast guards and port authorities of sovereign nations—in short, he made sure ships ran smoothly while they were in port, and made sure the crew had everything they needed.

He'd met Amaya when she had visited one of the ships her father worked on. King had been in the captain's cabin engrossed in the minutiae of some routine shipboard paperwork. He'd barely looked up when Amaya had swished in and hugged her father, the captain. He'd ignored their conversation, easy to do since he didn't understand the language, and it wasn't until he had a question about the form he was working on that he looked up and really saw her.

And when he did, he was smitten. Amaya was tall, had beautifully bronzed skin from her Iranian heritage, classically voluptuous, spoke fluent English and craved for travel, much like King.

James had stayed in Rotterdam longer than he had planned, and they had dated, slowly at first, coffee and lunch dates, movies and ice cream. When James finally had to leave, he was heartbroken and soon after arranged a sabbatical from work to free him to rejoin Amaya.

She waited for him, and when he returned, their love blossomed. Amaya was a sweet woman. It wasn't until America that she changed, was manipulated herself. They married in a small ceremony attended by close friends and family and set off together to travel to places neither one had ever been. It was like a honeymoon that never ended.

When money eventually got tight, James suggested they return to his home in Corpus Christi so that he could go back to work. He promised her they would still travel together at every opportunity.

However, when James returned, despite his best efforts, work took precedence. When he tried to carve some time out of his schedule, his company took advantage of his good nature and said they couldn't do without him. They gave him a significant raise, which made James feel as if he had to work harder to justify the extra money. He traveled all the time. Amaya accompanied him on some trips like he'd promised, but it wasn't the same. King was always working, so often she was left on her own and often in less than desirable ports, in less than desirable countries.

Amaya started staying at home more. Growing apart. And when King was home, he was always occupied with the next trip, or tired from traveling. The sex grew less frequent. Conversation dried up, became rote.

James didn't notice her mental absence at first, but by the time he did, he was on the road again, off to another port. Perhaps if he'd had some insight into what his job was doing to their marriage, he could have made changes. Demanded more time off, better ports to work out of, even quit. He was a good man, but like most men, he was blind to what was happening in front of him.

Amaya, bored and lonely, in a foreign country, unable to work, no close friends, was walking past a mosque one day when the music from within called to something in her soul. She wasn't a religious person, never had been, but something resonated inside her, and she entered the mosque.

It was an enlightening and rewarding experience for her, and she had a lot of free time to immerse herself in something she never knew was missing from her life. She read the Koran, listened to the teachings of the Imam, and could have gone on like this forever. That is, until she met Halil al-Majarifi.

al-Majarifi was charming, educated, and took an interest in Amaya. Something she was desperately missing from her husband. It didn't hurt that he was handsome, seemed well off, smelled good, and could converse fluently in Arabic..

al-Majarifi had observed Amaya in the mosque several times before. He noted she was always alone, had followed her home on occasion and confirmed her house was usually empty. She often looked lonely and at times sad, and it was easy for him to approach her and insinuate himself into her life. Sitting next to her, hands brushing accidentally as they both reached for the same prayer book. A shy look, a quick smile. Nodding and smiling at her as they passed in the street. A shared conversation with the Imam.

It was easy to suggest coffee. Perhaps they could talk about the Koran? He knew a place just around the corner. Amaya, with nothing else to do, and no one to go home to, didn't give it a second thought. For his part, al-Majarifi was well practiced in the subtle art of seduction. He'd done this enough times to perfect his art and was indeed trained for this. He was more than he let on to Amaya—at least to begin with—al-Majarifi was a Haqqani network recruiter. An operative whose sole goal was to manipulate people and convert them to his cause. He routinely visited mosques in the area, always on the lookout for new talent, people that he could take advantage of. And Amaya was ripe for the taking.

al-Majarifi fed her information one spoonful at a time. Grooming her. Over several months. It was a slow process, to be sure, but radicalization takes some time. Some of what he showed her was true, some not so true, some a slight manipulation of the truth to make US policies appear immoral and corrupt. It was easy to do. He upped the ante, showed her YouTube videos of purportedly American bombings and the destruction of schools and hospitals these caused. Mass civilian casualties. Videos of screaming mothers and burning children, whole villages decimated. All fake, but expertly crafted, and Amaya fell for it all. She had no close friends. Her family lived in another country, and her husband was gone more than he was ever home. al-Majarifi didn't need to separate Amaya from her support network; she didn't have one to begin with. It was a long game he was playing, and it wasn't happenstance that he picked Amaya.

She started to believe his lies. Her mind turned slowly from boredom to hatred, and her hatred turned to a wish to do something to help, to stop the American infidels.

Months of meetings, coffee breaks, and lunch dates gradually turned Amaya's affections from James to Halil.

James King kept on working, kept on traveling. Their sex life, once explorative and enthusiastic, wilted. Conversation went the same way. Amaya didn't care, and James, too tired from work and time zone changes, didn't notice.

Amaya fell deeply in love with al-Majarifi and completely swallowed the lies he was telling her. He showed her how she could use sex to manipulate men, to get what she wanted, not realizing that all the while, he was manipulating her. Amaya was an eager and willing student.

al-Majarifi was the one who asked Amaya to ensure that two new crew members got on board the *Supra Reliance*. He didn't say why, and Amaya never asked. She was only too happy to show al-Majarifi that she could do what he asked.

It was easy to influence King, and as they rarely had sex, it was all too easy to remind him of what was and what could be. She did this for al-Majarifi, she did this for herself, and she did this for her new beliefs.

King parked on Leopard Street near downtown, coincidentally just around the corner from Tower Two, slamming the car door and almost jogging into the building such was his haste. He waved at Lucy, the receptionist, punched the button for the elevator, watching it slowly descend from the twelfth to the eleventh floor, his patience wearing thin. When it didn't appear to have moved for more than a minute, King bolted for the stairs and ran up the four flights of stairs to his office. Need to work out more, he thought, huffing up the last flight.

He pulled a crumpled tissue from his back pocket and wiped his brow, clicked open the door to his office, sat down behind his desk, his gut jiggling a little, too many Big Mac's, he thought, and wiggled the mouse to wake the computer up.

Calling up the manifest for the *Supra Reliance*, he pulled out a post-it note from his pocket that Amaya had written the two names on. He glanced at it, smoothed it out in front of him on his desk and carefully typed the names exactly as they appeared into the ship's manifest. He sent the manifest via e-mail to the ship and CBP, waited for the 'e-mail sent' message to appear, logged out, and retraced his steps back to his car, this time pausing for the elevator.

"Blasted inconvenience, this is, chief," Captain Roberts said from the bridge of the *Supra Reliance*. "When did you say the two replacements were getting here?"

"Should be any minute. The shipping agent just sent me the new manifest. Has their names on it."

Roberts grunted. "I guess it's a good job only two of us went down from eating that dodgy salad. Could have had a real crisis on our hands if the whole crew had succumbed."

The chief officer shrugged and tapped out a cigarette from a Marlboro Red soft pack. Lighting it, he inhaled and blew out a stream of smoke, saying, "It was a stroke of luck that the shipping agent had two people ready to go. Said they just got off another ship in port and were willing to sail with us. Saves us from having to ask the Coast Guard to sail short, and best of all, we can keep to schedule."

Roberts watched from the bridge wing as two men approached on foot, sea bags slung over their shoulders. He could see them walk up the gangway and present identification to the watch stander.

"This must be them now, chief. Can you get them up to speed so we can shove off?" He looked at his watch. "I'd like to catch the next tide if we can, should be slack tide in about two hours. Plan for that if you could."

"Aye, sir." The chief officer left the bridge wing to meet his new crew.

The two new hires were qualified for their positions, but that wasn't the only reason they were on board. When the vessel left port, their real work could begin, and the two Haqqani network operatives would strike fear into the belly of the infidel beast.

King wasn't a dangerous man, wasn't evil, wasn't a big religious man, a fanatic of any kind, and he couldn't care less about what he'd just done.

All he knew was that he just wanted to have sex with his wife. Was that so wrong? He pushed his foot a little harder onto the accelerator, and the small car surged forward.

"Fuck. Fuck. Fuck," he said, as he saw blue lights in his rearview mirror. In his haste to dip his wick, he'd completely ignored the school zone speed limit sign he'd just passed. He briefly registered that the flashing speed limit sign said he was going fifty in a fifteen.

"Fuck," he said again. He eased over to the side of the road and put the car in park. He rolled down his window, turned the engine off, thumped the steering wheel, and waited for the officer. There was no chance he was going to get home now. At his speed, that was a felony.

Thirteen

"Frank, we may have something?" Smith said. It seemed more of a question than a statement. "What's up?" We'd come back to the office to review the evidence we had in case we'd missed anything. There wasn't much to go on. I was sitting at my makeshift desk, a cold mug of coffee slowly congealing from the cream, when Smith approached me.

"The local cops picked up this guy downtown for speeding through a school zone. The initial report from the patrol officer said he looked sweaty and nervous, more so than a usual stop would have made someone behave, so he ran his license and registration. Would have done anyway with how fast he was going."

"How fast?"

"About three times the speed limit."

I whistled. "Man, that's ballsy in a school zone. No one's hurt, right?"

"No, we're all good there, thankfully."

"Okay. I'm listening."

"So, the license check didn't come back with anything interesting on this guy per se, although he's a shipping agent downtown which may become relevant later, I don't know. Anyway, the reason this guy got on our radar is because the FBI asked local LE to let them know if anything interesting popped up concerning him. The arresting officer didn't know if this counted as interesting but figured it wouldn't hurt to run it up the chain. Don't be the highest-ranking person with a secret and all that."

"What's his name?"

"James King," Smith continued, "but it's not him the FBI are interested in, it's his spouse, Amaya King. Allegedly she's sympathetic to a terrorist organization called the Haqqani network."

"Never heard of them."

"Me either. But I did some quick digging. Apparently, they're based out of Afghanistan, have a few small training camps for local yahoos, similar interests as the Taliban and hate all things western."

"Nothing new then."

"No, it's the same broken record. Anyway, the feds have had their eye on a guy called al-Majarifi. He hangs out at different mosques in our area and tries to convert people to his cause. Which, of course, is general hate and discontent. King's wife is someone the feds believe he's converted."

"You're thinking he may have a connection to our two unsubs?"

"I think it's possible. Shipping agent and a terrorist connection, it may pan out into something."

"Why don't the feds take him off the street if they know this al-Majarifi is citing violence?"

"You know how it is. If they keep tabs on him and under observation they can find his new converts, who they can also keep an eye on. Then they can take down a whole terrorist cell, not just one person. That's how they found this King." Smith turned the pages in his notepad and shrugged. "They like him where he is, better the devil you know and all that."

"Okay, but how does this tie in with anything we've got going on?"

"I'm getting to that." He paused. "You know, before I get too far down the rabbit trail, let's adjourn to my office. Why don't you get Carter and meet me there in five?"

"Sure." I stood up, went to the galley, dumped my coffee, thought about pouring some more, but decided to rinse the cup first, and then poured some.

I didn't know how much airedale coffee I could sneak as the airport building was damn near ready for us to move in. Amazing what a little fire and brimstone will do to speed up the wheels of government.

I walked up to Carter's desk. "Hey, Jess. Smith wants us in his office. He might have a lead on the case, something about a shipping agent and a terrorist cell."

She looked at me and raised an eyebrow but didn't say anything and followed me to his office, really a small lieutenant's closet he'd commandeered for the time being. We squeezed in, and I tried to close the door.

"Don't bother with the door," Smith said. "It doesn't close properly."

Never one to leave a challenge unanswered, I managed to wrestle the door closed anyway, and we stood in the cramped space as there was nowhere to sit.

"So, I gave Frank the basic details," Smith said, looking at Carter, "but the feds have a James King in custody. He was speeding when the cops pulled him over, acting more nervous than he should be. However, at this point, we really don't care about him, we're more interested in his wife. She has connections to the Haqqani network—"

"Terrorist group out of Afghanistan, right? Hates our guts, wants to kill us all?" Carter said.

"Right." Smith looked at her for a moment, appraising her. "Neither Frank nor I had heard of them until just now."

"I was doing some light reading the other day about terrorist groups," she shrugged. "They popped up."

I shook my head. Sometimes she just amazed me.

"Sure. Here's the thing," Smith continued, clearing his throat. "King is a shipping agent. His wife is an associate of a known terrorist recruiter. The feds pulled King in; they want to grill him. See what his wife's been up to, see if he's involved in any way.

"We haven't got any other leads, we don't know what's going on, except that there are some very dangerous individuals running around our town. I want you two to join the FBI's interrogation team and see if this King spills anything that might help us. I'm tired of operating in the dark. This may get us into the light. Any questions?"

We both shook our heads.

"Then get to it."

The FBI ran a satellite office in Corpus Christi located on North Shoreline Boulevard in the One Shoreline Plaza building, not so far, as it happens, from the T-Heads where I docked *Serenity*. The place was a monster of concrete and glass, rising in two separate towers to twenty-eight and twenty-two floors, respectively. It was the tallest building in South Texas, south of San Antonio. The two towers—Corpus Christi building planners must like to keep things in two's—connected to each other with an impressive walkway and command a stunning view of the bay from every floor. The FBI was in the north tower, the shorter one, on the eleventh floor, which still rose three hundred and seventy-five feet into the air.

Truth be told, if the two fucktards had blown this place up instead of my Tower Two, it would have made much more of an impact, so to speak. But my Tower Two was showing its age, whereas this place had all the bells and whistles, electronic surveillance systems, cameras, secure doors, and 24-hour security, so it probably would have been much harder. Besides, the Coast Guard wasn't here in this shiny place but tucked away around the corner, so I guess they achieved their result after all.

We parked in the adjacent covered lot and walked through a corridor coming out into the lobby.

"Man," I said, looking around. "We sure are in the wrong business."

The entire lobby was wall to ceiling glass, and our shoes echoed off the polished marble floors, which were so shiny I could have parted my hair in the reflection.

"Excuse me, sir," I said to the security guard stationed behind the lobby desk. He was in his fifties and wearing a tidy black polo shirt with a security badge emblazoned on the left breast of his shirt. "Agents Dalton and Carter here for the FBI."

He looked at our badges and then at our faces and, seemingly satisfied, said, "They're in the north tower, eleventh floor. Cut across the lobby to the north tower and take the blue elevators to eleven."

I thanked him, and we walked off, admiring the potted palms, the intense air conditioning keeping us cool even with the sun shining down on all the glass, and just the general feel-good flavor of the place.

Carter hit the call button for the elevator, and I tried lightening the mood by complaining in a high-pitched kids voice that I had wanted to mash the button, so now it meant I had dibs to hit the floor button when we were inside the elevator. She didn't smile.

The FBI had a swish office. All glass and chrome, not like the usual dreary outposts of concrete and spray stucco. This must have been a great PR gig for someone. Maybe they did some recruiting videos here.

The reception desk held a perky thirty-something receptionist with a chopstick wedged into her bun to keep her hair in place. She was perched behind a desk, on which rested a phone and a large monitor along with the usual desk paraphernalia. I announced our presence, and she picked up the phone, dialed a 4-digit extension and spoke quietly into it.

"Someone will be right out," she said, ghosting me a smile and looking Carter up and down.

I thanked her, and within a minute a tall, slim lady, made taller by her four-inch heels, came out to meet us from behind one of the glass office doors. She wore a red skirt, cut just above the knee, and an off-white, short-sleeved blouse, tastefully tight but not too revealing. Her hair was some sort of blonde shade and tied in an efficient bun. I could see a necklace, the pendant drawing my eyes where they shouldn't go, and she held a pleasant and expectant smile, small button nose, full lips, sharp blue eyes, and cute ears. I know, ears, right? What can I say? I like ears.

"Agents," she said, her voice breathing life into the smile she had. "My name is Special Agent Tanya Williams, welcome to the FBI. Please, follow me, and I'll brief you."

We shook hands and followed. She closed the glass door behind us, lowering the blinds for some privacy.

"That's impressive," Carter said, staring out the window. "How on earth do you get any work done with that view?"

Williams looked out the window as if seeing it for the first time in a long time.

"Please sit." She gestured to two comfortable-looking chairs across from her desk and perched herself on the edge, ensuring the skirt remained respectable. "It is rather impressive, isn't it? You know, I suppose it's like anything, you just tune it out after a while. A bit of a shame." She shrugged. "Now, how much do you know?"

"Our ASAC, Tobias Smith, told us you had a Mr. King in custody and that it's his wife you're interested in, that she's been radicalized."

"Good. That's it in a nutshell. We have him on the other side of the office; this entire floor is ours. We even have our own back entrance, useful for days like this when we bring suspects in. So far, he's been cooperative as he thinks he's in deep shit for excessively speeding in a school zone. We haven't started interrogating him yet and haven't asked him anything about his wife. Interestingly enough, he didn't ask why the FBI was involved in a speeding ticket, so perhaps he knows more than he's letting on."

"He hasn't asked for a lawyer?" I asked.

"Nope. And we hope he keeps it that way. His mistake is our gain, although if we had to, we could probably book him under the Patriot Act for aiding and abetting a known terrorist sympathizer. That would keep the lawyers away for a few days."

"What about his wife?"

"That's the problem. We only had intermittent surveillance on her. As soon as King left for work this morning, she took off. Our guy lost her, so she's in the wind for now. We don't believe the husband is involved, but he might know where she was going or what she was up to. How do you want to play this?"

I thought for a minute. "Listen, don't take this the wrong way, but I think it might work better if both of you go in together, without me," I said. "If the guy loves women, he might open up to you, and if he hates women, it might throw him off track a little." I shrugged. "I think it's worth a shot. Lay it out about his wife. How she's been cheating on him, and then with who. If he knows anything, it might make him angry enough to spill."

"Or make him so sad he doesn't want to talk."

"Then don't let him get sad."

I watched through the two-way mirror as Carter and Williams walked in. King glanced at them as they approached the steel desk. He looked down, eyes subdued as they sat down across from him.

"Mr. King," Williams began. "My name is Special Agent Williams. This is Special Agent Carter. Do you know why you're here today?"

He shrugged.

"You don't think it's unusual that the FBI took custody from the local police, just for a speeding ticket?"

He shrugged again.

"Come on, Mr. King. You must have some idea that this is unusual?"

He finally raised his head, eyes flickering between the two, with a look of not quite defiance, but almost resignation. "It was a school zone."

Williams paused for a moment, assessing. "And that warrants an FBI investigation? Come on, King, you look like an intelligent man. You must know that can't be all of it." She leaned forward, looking him in the eye. "If you 'fess up now, to what you know, it'll be a hell of a lot easier on you. We know what you did. Why don't you just confirm it for us, and then we can get you out of here. We can even waive the moving violation."

A bead of sweat slowly dripped down the side of King's face. "I'm not sure what you mean. I was just speeding." Then he added, "allegedly."

"Okay. Do it the hard way. I was trying to give you an easy out." She pushed a folder over to him. "Open it."

King leaned forward. Hesitantly, as if this might be a trap of some sort he hadn't fathomed, he flipped the folder open.

"What's this?"

"What does it look like?"

"It looks like a blurry photo of my wife. Where did you get this? What has this got to do with my speeding?" He coughed. "Allegedly speeding."

This guy was a riot. Carter and Williams glanced at each other. Was he really this dumb, or just playing? If he was playing, he was at the top of his game.

Carter said, "James. My name's Jessica. Can I call you James?"

King nodded. Carter continued. "Not a great day so far, is it?" King shrugged. "We really want to get you on your way, James, but we need your help. Where were you going in such a rush?"

"Home."

"And what's at home, James?"

"My wife."

"Okay. That's good, James. Really helpful. So, you were on the way home to your wife...Why don't you take another look at the folder, James?"

King picked up the folder and started to leaf through, studying them this time. I knew what was there. I'd seen them before they went into the interrogation room. He was looking at multiple images of his wife—in the mosque, in a café with al-Majarifi, getting cozy with al-Majarifi, and finally, some grainy images of his wife getting intimate, again with al-Majarifi.

His hands shook, his face red. He put the photos back down. "Can I...Can I get a glass of water please?"

"Sure. In a minute, James," Carter said. "Why don't you tell me about these photos?"

"I can't. It must be AI. She would never. I—" He coughed, wracking, heaving coughs that subsided into shaking, crying.

I guess he didn't know. When he'd calmed down some, Carter offered him a tissue.

He blew his nose loudly, accepting another tissue from Carter. He mumbled his thanks. "Are these real?" he said eventually, tapping the folder.

Williams and Carter both nodded.

"I'm not sure I believe you," he said, but you could tell he did. He looked beat. "Who's the man?"

Williams sighed. "I'm sorry, James. Your wife is involved in some bad shit," she said. "She's been going to a mosque, for several months. Nothing wrong with that, it probably started innocently enough in the beginning, but this guy," she thumbed through the photos and tapped one of al-Majarifi, "found her. He's a terrorist recruiter for the Haqqani network. He manipulated her and recruited her."

King sniffled. "He's a what? The who? No, not my Ami. I don't believe it. I—"

Carter reached across the table for his hand, trying to show empathy. "It's all true, James. What we need to know is how much you know. I believe you're not involved, James, but we have to make sure."

"So, this...this isn't about speeding?" He looked up, finally realizing what a world of shit he might be in. "Am I in trouble? I think I may want to call a lawyer." He did look a bit ashen.

"You can certainly call your lawyer if you wish, James, but right now, we're trying to understand what your wife has been up to. We believe that there's a terrorist cell working locally, and your wife, however peripherally, may be involved. Time really is of the essence. A lawyer will only slow down the truth, and that could lead to a lot of people dying." Carter paused for a moment to let that sink in. "You don't want innocent people to die James, do you? Not if you could stop these terrorists, surely."

King sighed and rubbed his face, smearing a trail of snot along his upper lip. "I don't know anything. Seriously. I don't know anything about terrorists, I'm a shipping agent for Christ's sake. If my wife, like you say, which I'm still not sure of, has been doing these things, I never knew. I travel a lot. I suppose..."

"It often starts out that way, James," Williams said. "There was probably nothing you could have done to stop this. This al-Majarifi is an expert at manipulation. Your wife, once he locked onto her, didn't stand a chance. It really wasn't her fault, you know? If you're looking to blame someone, blame this guy. He probably doesn't even like your wife. He just wants to convert her to his cause. It's a big game for him. She's the ultimate victim."

King nodded. "I guess. What...what will happen to her?"

"Well, that depends, James," Carter said. "Did she ask you to do anything? Ask you to deliver something to somebody, perhaps? A small package? We know you're a shipping agent, did she ask you to put something on board a ship? A small bag she wouldn't let you open, but that was unusually heavy? Said it was a gift for the captain, an old friend, something like that?"

King was caught between a rock and a hard place. While I felt sorry for the guy, he could be the link we were looking for. His life would go on, but maybe others wouldn't. We needed to know.

"No. No, nothing like that. No packages, no deliveries. I can't believe this. We were going to have sex after I got back from work."

"Is that why you were speeding, James? Rushing to get back home to get laid," Willams said.

King nodded. "Yeah."

Of all the lucky breaks. "Where were you coming from, James?" Carter asked. "What were you doing? Was it something that Amiya had asked you to do? Was it a delivery?"

A whirlwind of emotions fluttered across his face. Anger, humiliation, disbelief, finally settling on glum.

"You know the sex was never going to happen, James, don't you," Williams said, then softer, "I'm sorry. I hate to tell you this, but Amiya left your house shortly after you drove off. Did you know that? Do you know where she is?"

"Do I know...? I don't even know *who* she is. Fuck."

"James. Where did you go? What did Amiya ask you to do for her?" Carter said.

"Can I have another tissue, please?" King said. Carter pushed over the box, and King took one and blew his nose again. He cleared his throat. "I went to work. I had to update the crew manifest, add...Amaya wanted me to...shit." He leaned forward, understanding finally crossing his face. "I know what it was." He sat up straighter in his chair and rubbed his face. "Fuuuuck. I didn't really think anything of it at the time. Man, she had me wrapped around her finger. Listen, I end up making last minute changes all the time, if I'd known she was being manipulated, I would never have done what she asked."

Behind the screen, I was bursting. Answer the question, man.

"It wasn't a package she wanted me to deliver. It was names."

Williams and Carter glanced at each other. "Names?" Carter asked. "What do you mean?"

King shook his head. "Look, I understand I'm in some trouble, and there might be some bad actors in the area, but if I tell you what I know, I want some sort of guarantee."

Williams spoke. "Maybe we can work something out, James. It depends on what you tell us."

King hesitated. "Okay. Okay. You must know I would never do anything to hurt anyone."

"We know that, James," Carter said. "Tell us what you did."

"I added two crew names to the manifest of the *Supra Reliance*. It's an oil tanker. It's in port to load with crude, should be getting underway soon."

"What were the names you added, James?"

I took a moment to process this information as he recited the names and then burst into the room. King looked startled, but I didn't care. "Carter, let's go. Tanya, meet us at the ship. Everyone you can spare, full tactical gear."

I pulled out my phone, running for the elevator. "Tobias? We've got it. King added two names to the *Supra Reliance* manifest. The ship is still in port. It has to be the two we're looking for. We'll meet you there, everything we've got. All of it. Bring it."

Fourteen

I'd had a minor epiphany on the way to the tanker. We'd game-planned over the phone with Smith and the FBI while Carter drove. We didn't know what these two had gotten on board for. Had they planted bombs? Taken the crew hostage? Hidden among the many squirrel holes on board a ship?

Instead of a full-out frontal assault—the plan I had initially wanted—we were going to err on the side of caution. This was a massive oil tanker loaded with product slap bang in the middle of the port. If we fucked this up and the terrorist motherfuckers put their plan into action, at the very least, there could be an environmental impact that would blow away the damage the *Exxon Valdez* had done. I didn't want the name of the *Supra Reliance* to be synonymous with a botched operation from the Coast Guard.

We decided on a more rational scenario. Carter and I, along with armed Coasties from the enforcement department of the Sector, were going on board. There would be six of us. We'd assume the roles of a team conducting a Port State boarding, routine for all foreign vessels. We could check the crew documents, nose around the ship, check spaces and hopefully get the drop on these guys. It was unusual to conduct a boarding right before a ship left port, but not without precedent, so hopefully we wouldn't raise too many eyebrows.

We strode up the gangway as if we owned it. Backup was beyond the proverbial hill, lying in wait, with gnashing of teeth and clashing of arms. All we had to do was yell.

A bored Philippine crewmember bounced to attention when he saw us come aboard. Check IDs, yes, sir. Sign book, yes, sir. Captain in his cabin, follow me.

We gathered in his cabin. I could see the captain knew something wasn't quite right. We were armed, but that wasn't unusual. I think he must have picked up on the body language.

"Cap," I said. "We're here to conduct a routine boarding on your vessel. Could you have someone bring up all your passports and mariner credentials up here please?"

He hesitated a second but then nodded and barked something unintelligible to a crewmember lurking in the corner of the room, who jumped as if a thousand volts of electricity had been rammed up his ass.

The captain was an old salt. Big whispery beard, tinged with streaks of white, but yellowing around the mouth. He wore a ball cap on his head, oily around the brim. His arms were free of tattoos and poked out from a sweat-stained white shirt.

"Coffee?" he said.

I spoke for the team. "No thanks, Cap. If it's okay with you, my team would like to start in the engine room, while we wait," I pointed between Carter and me, "for the documents."

He nodded, picked up the phone and yelled into it. A moment later, a short man in grease-stained coveralls reeking of body odor appeared.

The captain rattled off some fast-paced language, and the engineer beckoned to whoever was going to follow him.

"Good luck, guys. Let me know."

They nodded and left with the engineer. A moment later, the first crew member appeared with a box of papers.

"Captain, what is this, the documents you asked for."

"Thanks, Sandy," he said, and handed a large white binder to me.

"Fantastic," I said. "May we?"

We sat down at the captain's conference table, and I started going through the passports and ship documents. It wasn't long before I came across the two we were looking for. I identified them by virtue of they'd come aboard today. The question was, how was I going to play this? I could ask the captain what he knew, take him into my confidence, and explain why we were here or play it by ear. The thing was, I didn't know if the captain was in on it. I glanced at Carter, looking for some help. She shrugged.

I sighed.

Fuck it.

"Cap, can you sit down for a minute, I need to discuss something with you." I glanced at the crewmember standing at attention by the door. "In private."

The captain looked at me oddly but caught my drift.

"Sandy, give us some privacy, please. Why don't you see if you can rustle up some bottles of water?"

Sandy nodded and left. I thought I could hear him saying, what is this.

The captain sat, looked at us, and raised his bushy eyebrows.

I let out a breath and dove in. Here goes nothing, I thought. "Cap, these two men," I showed him the passports of the two terrorists. "Have you noticed anything unusual about them since they came aboard?"

He studied the passports and handed them back. "No. They only came aboard a few hours ago. What have they done?"

Shit. "Nothing?" I said.

He studied me for a moment. This was a shrewd guy. What was his game?

"Since," he said, emphasizing the word, "they came aboard. I have not noticed anything unusual, nor have there been reports from any of my crew about anything unusual either. But they have only been on board a few hours. Is there something I should know about them?"

Time to lay it on the line. "Cap, these two men are suspected terrorists. Anything you can tell me will help us capture them and prevent any potential catastrophe or casualties on board this vessel."

His eyes opened a fraction. "Terrorists?"

"Yes. Linked to the Haqqani network."

"Afghanistan?" he said.

I nodded. Did everyone know but me? The captain stood up and walked to his desk. He stood there for a moment. I could see his chest heaving, and then his right hand lashed out and swept away whatever was on top, ashtray, glasses, books. All of it clattered to the deck.

Sandy raced in at the noise and received a verbal thrashing from the captain. Sandy hightailed it back out.

The captain walked back to the conference table and sat down again.

"I apologize for my outburst. I know the Haqqani. They are evil, vicious bastards. Dogs. Curs. Vile beings," he paused for a breath. I thought he was going to spit on the floor, but he didn't. "Forgive me. I thought you came here to harass my crew. It's unusual for a boarding right before sailing.

"I have not seen anything suspicious with these two since they have been aboard. They have been quiet, but that is always normal for new crew. However, their manner of arriving was unusual. Two of my crew got sick last night unexpectedly, and these two were here this morning. It's unusual to get qualified replacements so quickly." He shrugged. "Of course, I cannot run without a full crew. The Coast Guard, you know, are sticklers for manning requirements," he smiled, "so it was most welcome that we received notice of replacements. No reason to suspect they were terrorists."

I leaned forward. "Where are they now, cap? We don't know what they're doing on board. We have teams at the ready but want to take them down quietly and without trouble, if we can."

He nodded. "Of course. I'll just call the chief—"

A rolling ball of fire roared through the captain's door, breaking it off its hinges, followed by the shock wave. Or was it the shockwave first, followed by the rolling ball of fire? In the instant of the explosion, I was launched across the room. Carter and the captain went with me. I saw smoke, smelled fire, or was that smelled smoke and saw fire? Was I on fire? My brain was ringing and up was down. I was lying on my back, and I could see an arm resting across my chest. I tried to move it, but it wouldn't budge. Oh, fuck, I'm paralyzed.

I struggled to sit up, and the arm slid off my chest. Oh, fucking fuck, I've lost my arm.

The arm moved. I looked at my hands. It wasn't mine. Carter had landed beside me, and it was her arm I'd dislodged. Man, that did a number on my head.

"Jess. You okay?" I was yelling as the sound of the explosion had affected my hearing.

She groaned and rolled over. She looked banged up, but I couldn't see anything major. I ran my hands over her but didn't feel any broken bones, nor did I see any blood. I looked around for the captain. He wasn't looking so hot. A steel skewer, like you use for kebabs, was impaled improbably through his left eyeball. He wasn't moving. Where the fuck had that skewer come from?

I crawled over to him and gave him a light shake. Nothing. I checked his pulse. No response. Fuck again.

"I think they know we're here, Jess."

"Ugh. You think?"

"You okay? Good to go?" My hearing was coming back.

"Let's toast the bitches," she said, easing herself off the deck.

Toast the bitches? I looked around for the portable radio but couldn't see it. The enforcement guys may not have heard the blast if they were in the engine room, but that couldn't be helped. Hopefully they felt motion from the concussion, but I couldn't count on it.

I drew my weapon and headed out the hole that used to be the door.

We had two men to hunt. They could be anywhere. Apparently, they had access to explosives, but what else?

We raced down the corridor. Sandy lay on the deck, a knife sticking out of his chest. I stopped for a moment to check his pulse, but there was nothing. I pulled the knife out, thinking it might come in useful, wiping the blood off on his shirt. Sorry. I knew it was evidence, but I felt I had a better need for the knife than Sandy did.

I stopped at the door to the outside deck. "Up or down?" I said.

"It would be easier if we knew what they were trying to do. If they were scuttling the ship, I'd say down. If they're trying to take over, I'd say up, to the bridge. Fuck, maybe both, maybe they're just going to leave."

"I don't think they're trying to leave. They could have done that without trying to blow us up." I scrubbed my face and checked my Glock. "Let's go up. Maybe we can find a radio and hail the reinforcements. Not much point in holding back now."

Carter nodded, and we slipped out the door to the outside deck. Spying a ladder in front of us, I kept my eyes peeled and ran toward it and up. Carter had my six, and I could hear her footsteps on the metal rungs right behind me.

The bridge appeared before me, the door wedged open with a block of wood. I nodded to Carter and slid into the room, going low while she came in high. If the fuckers were in here, they couldn't take us both out.

Bending at the waist, gun drawn, I entered the bridge and scanned the room. Empty. It should have had at least one or two people on duty, even in port.

"Get on the radio, Jess. Call the army."

I looked out the bridge windows, half listening to her in the background, and looked across the vast deck of the ship. Nothing seemed amiss.

"They're on their way. All the exits to the port facility have been blocked. There's no way out."

"I don't think that's going to bother them. Okay," I took a moment to think. "They're not up here. Maybe they planned on scuttling this bastard at the dock? It'd block the channel for months."

"Engine room," we both said at once.

Ignoring the possibility that one of the Haqqani may have been lying in wait—stupid maybe, but we didn't have time to spare—we raced back down the ladder, back inside the superstructure and down a mountain's worth of stairs.

It wouldn't be easy to scuttle this beast, but a few well-placed explosives on the sea chest and placed around the skin of the hull would do the trick. I hoped the enforcement team was okay.

As I opened the outer door to the engine room, the noise blasted at me. With no time to mess with hearing protection, I yanked open the inner door. The smell of grease and diesel wrapped around me like a bear hug from an old lost friend. I glanced at Carter, motioning for her to go left while I went right.

The engine room was massive, and it needed to be to house the engine. A single-screw, low-speed diesel engine was in the middle of the space, easily four decks high. And did I mention loud?

Lots of places to hide, and I had to be cognizant that there were probably friendly crew in here along with our team. Couldn't shoot everyone that popped up—much as I wanted to.

I had little reason for stealth. No one was going to hear me coming, but on the flip side, I couldn't hear anybody either.

I went down one deck, and I lost sight of Carter. As I crept around a corner, I caught a glimmer of something in my peripheral vision. I ducked on instinct. That probably saved my life.

A massive wrench, at least three feet long, slammed into a steel frame—narrowly missing the space recently vacated by my head. No way would I have survived that.

The fucker holding the wrench, a big boy, was already reeling back for another swing, but he was slow. I charged him, going low under his swing and caught him in the stomach and kept running, keeping him off balance. He tried to smash the wrench into my back but only succeeded in a glancing blow. I staggered but kept pushing until I felt us stop. I'd pushed him into the railing. It was designed to prevent idiots from falling three decks, and I had his back wedged against the upper rail.

I took a step back, ducked another wild swing, and kicked his knee out. He grimaced but didn't go down. I grabbed his wrist that held the wrench with my left hand and punched him in the throat with my right. He dropped the wrench on reflex and brought his hands to his neck, gasping for breath. I ducked low and tried to scoop up his feet. He kicked out, catching me in the shoulder, and I stumbled back landing on the deck. He bent down to pick up the wrench, took a couple of steps and swung at my head again. I scooted backward just in time and could feel the wrench reverberate through the deck plating as it hit the floor.

I'd dropped my pistol during the scuffle, and I scanned the deck for it while getting back to my feet. The fucker was coming at me again, so I went in low, power driving my shoulder into his gut, ducking his swing. He was off balance, and I shoved him harder into the railing. Keeping my momentum going, I wrapped both arms around the back of his knees and deadlifted him, using the railing at his back as a makeshift hinge. His eyes widened, and he dropped the wrench, windmilling his arms in an attempt to defy gravity.

His bulk was his death sentence, and as soon as his upper body went past the point of no return, he fell, a look of pure terror on his face.

His mouth was open, but his scream was silenced by the noise in the engine room. I watched dispassionately as his head exploded like a dropped watermelon on a piece of exposed machinery a deck down, the rest of his body falling lifeless into the bilge.

One down.

I found my pistol wedged underneath a tool cabinet, pried it loose and then leaned against the rail, heart pounding, sweat pouring from the exertion and heat in the engine room. I heard shots, or I thought I heard what sounded like shots, difficult to tell in here, and ran in that direction.

Nothing on this deck, so I went down one more. I caught a glimpse of Carter through the deck grating below me. She was about fifty feet ahead of me and running fast. I couldn't see who she was chasing, but it had to be the other guy.

I vaulted over the railing, praying there was nothing below to get impaled on. Halfway down, just as I saw I'd land clear, I was blown back by a small explosion. The air rushed out of me as I fell flat on my back, the deck grating flaying my skin as I skidded.

"Carter," I yelled. I got back on my feet, unsteady and groggy. The adrenaline kicked in even more, masking my pain, and I ran as best I could toward where I had last seen her.

She was covered in small burns, her clothes still smoking. It didn't look like she'd broken anything that I could see, but there was a rapidly swelling, angry looking knot on her forehead. And she wasn't moving.

"No, no, no." I fell to my knees beside her and checked her pulse. Nothing.

"Come on, Jess."

I moved my fingers an inch on her throat and caught a beat. Then another one. Alive.

I sat back on my haunches for a second, relief flooding through me, then remembering where I was, sprang up. My back screamed in protest, and I nearly went back down. I grabbed Carter's weapon from her holster—I'd lost mine when I fell—and stumbled toward the source of the explosion.

Through the smoke, I could see the bomb had cracked several raw water pipes, and water was spraying into the engine room. Slumped over one of the pipes was a man dressed in coveralls. He wasn't moving. I prodded him in the kidneys with the barrel of Carter's pistol, but he didn't budge.

I holstered the weapon so I could use both hands and pulled him from the pipe and onto the deck where I could get a good look at his face.

I mentally matched him to the photo from his documents. It wasn't him. It wasn't the other terrorist. This man must have been a crewmember. I crouched down and felt for a pulse, but unlike Carter, he wasn't so lucky. The explosion must have pulverized his insides to mush.

I was torn. I needed to help Carter, I didn't know how bad she was, or how much time she might have left. I also needed to search for this other guy, to stop him from trying to sink the ship. The few cracked pipes were an issue if left unattended, but an engineer should be able to shore up the pipes and close the valves. The terrorist wasn't done yet, not by a long shot.

In the end, I decided I had to help Carter. The cavalry was on the way, the enforcement guys were somewhere on board, and the port exits were all blocked. I made my way back to her. She was still out cold. I didn't want to leave her but didn't want to manhandle her up the stairs if she had internal injuries. I needed a stretcher and some help.

Mindful that water was still pouring into the engine room, I followed the catwalk to the engine control room, hoping someone was still alive inside.

"Hey," I said. Three figures were sitting in chairs, their backs to me. "Hey, I need some help here."

I grabbed the closest man to me and spun his chair around, angry that he wasn't moving. How dare he just sit there.

As I spun his chair, his head lolled back, exposing his slashed neck.

"Fuck." I checked the other two. One was stabbed, and with the other I couldn't tell what was wrong with him besides he was dead.

"Where the fuck are the enforcement guys?"

I saw a stretcher in the corner, grabbed it, and half-dragged half-carried it back to Carter. This would have been way easier with two people. I placed the stretcher next to her and, as carefully as I could, manhandled her onto the stretcher, securing her with the attached straps. I dragged her back to the ladder, but there was no way I was going to get her up by myself. I had to go for help.

I didn't know whether she could hear me or not, but I yelled I would be right back and to sit tight. Even now, I had jokes. Must be my coping mechanism.

I was halfway up the ladder when I saw black boots coming down and I pulled Carter's weapon from my holster with my free hand.

As I was about to say, freeze, I saw the barrel of the MEs gun and the blue Coast Guard uniform. I holstered the weapon with relief.

"Hey, give me a hand," I yelled up.

"What the fuck happened?" the ME shouted over the engine roar, looking at Carter.

"Doesn't matter," I shouted back. "Listen, one of the terrorists is still down here somewhere. There're at least four dead crew members. Consider him armed and very dangerous. The vessel is taking on water, so we need a damage control team down here to shore it up, and we need to get Agent Carter out of here as quickly as possible."

He signaled two of his men, and they grabbed the stretcher and maneuvered her up the ladder and went topside. The rest of the team went in search of the missing terrorist. I followed Carter's stretcher as they carried her through the ship and then down the gangway and to a waiting ambulance. Once I saw she was in good hands, I rallied myself, ignoring my back once again, and headed back to the gangway.

"Frank," Smith said from right behind me. "Where do you think you're going?"

I motioned toward the gangway, "I have to help. There's one of the fuckers left."

He shook his head. "Have you even seen your back? The only place you're going is on that ambulance with Carter. Let everyone else handle this one."

I was about to throw a, "But, sir," out there, but as the adrenaline wore off the pain in my back increased and I realized he was probably right. Besides, now there was a steady stream of FBI and ATF emblazoned jackets running up the gangway, so I'm sure the alphabet team would get it sorted out.

Fifteen

It'd been a few days since we'd cleared the ship. The enforcement team had found the other terrorist. They'd subdued him as he was working on securing a package to another raw water pipe. He was handed over to the FBI, but so far hadn't said a word. A bomb disposal tech had defused the package, which turned out to be a crude explosive, although it would have done some severe damage. We were lucky this time.

The onboard damage control team had stopped the flooding, but the tanker was still tied up until the FBI finished with their investigation. King's wife was still in the wind, but they'd issued a BOLO, and it would hopefully only be a matter of time before she was caught.

No one had found my gun yet, either. It'd probably show up at the next hull inspection, stuck in the bilge somewhere, or for sale on eBay.

Carter didn't have any internal injuries, just a mild concussion from the knot on her head, and a few singed areas that would heal. She was admitted overnight for observation, but they'd kicked her out the next day, saying to get some rest, take a couple of days off. Take a few vitamin Ms for pain as needed. The usual.

My back lacerations ended up with a few bandages and a tetanus shot, again nothing major. They didn't even admit me. We were the lucky ones, the survivors. The unlucky ones were the poor bastards on board that the Haqqani had taken out. They wouldn't be coming back. Neither would Miner nor Browning, but we'd stopped the terrorists from destroying the ship and shutting down the port. With all the oil on board the *Supra Reliance* had loaded, if spilled, would have caused an environmental catastrophe that would have been way worse than the *Exxon Valdez* ever was.

The media were running the story, but we were trying to keep a tight lid on what really happened. If the truth got out, the public would run around in a mass panic, which would serve the terrorist plan. Perhaps when the guy they'd caught was put on trial, the truth could come out. However, it was just as likely he'd end up in a tropical cage in Guantanamo Bay. Whatever.

I'd taken a couple of days off, tending to the always ongoing maintenance of *Serenity*, my back sore and a little stiff, and felt like I should catch up with Pete and have a beer or three. Carter had promised me she'd come sailing the next day, so I was at a loose end for now.

I could hear the dull whump whump whump of heavy-duty bass vibrating through the windows way before I walked up to Pete's bar. I stopped for a second, curious, wondering if I was in the wrong place. I cast an eye around me, looking back. T-Heads. Check. Cheesy palms in oversized pots outside, intermingling with cheap garden furniture, offering an outside escape from the gloom that was synonymous with Pete's bar. Check and check.

I was definitely in the right place. What threw me off was the loudness and choice of music. Pete was nothing if not a creature of habit. Music, though not precisely forbidden in his bar, wasn't encouraged in any great shape or form. If music was playing, it was some sort of light jazz coming from a dented Bluetooth speaker perched amongst the liquor bottles.

Like I said, Pete didn't go in for music much, and no one seemed to care either. That was part of the quirky charm of the old place. As I stood outside the bar's tinted glass door, I was all but being pushed back into the parking lot by the invisible force of sound waves.

I pulled open the door and was immediately assaulted by the deafening roar of song lyrics, the low-pitched bass boom, throbbing and pulsing, rattling my ribs, shaking the glasses perched behind the bar.

I held my hands over my ears. There was no one else in the bar except for Pete, a huge grin on his face.

"Pete! What the fuck is this noise? For Christ's sake, turn it down," I shouted at him.

He waved and said something I didn't catch over the noise. I risked taking one hand off my ear and mimed a twisting motion, slamming my hand back over my ear.

"Turn it the fuck down."

He caught the motion and picked up a gigantic remote from the top of the bar and pointed it at a gleaming piece of chrome and smoked glass, mounted prominently on a wall. The music lowered enough that I could hear myself think.

"That's much better," I said. I walked to the bar and perched on a stool, waiting for him to explain. He wore a too loud Hawaiian shirt with tiny pink embroidered flamingos, which were upside down, sideways, and right side up. The collar was open one too many buttons, and a tuft of gray-black hair poked out. He was well built, and despite being down in the brutal Texas heat for so long, his skin wasn't leathery and wrinkly like so many aging sun worshipers.

He still had a grin on his face. "You don't like?"

"I don't know, I couldn't think it was so loud. What is that God awful song you're playing, and why?"

Pete shrugged, still grinning, came around the bar, and motioned for me to follow him over to the gleaming music box next to the wall.

"Wanted to try something new, something different," he said.

"Aren't you too old for a mid-life crisis?"

"This is no crisis. This is brilliance. I can't believe I was missing out on so much culture. This, my friend," he swept his hand over the top of the chrome thing, almost lovingly, "this is the best sound system money can buy."

I arched an eyebrow at him, skeptical.

"Well, the best that my money can buy. I had a guy come in the other day and hooked it all up. I have enough amps and woofers, tweeters and watts to run a nightclub and power a small substation."

"Do even know what all that means?"

"Not a clue, buddy, but I don't need to know, I have a remote," he said, waving it at me. "Anyway, that music you heard was the great Cardi B. Isn't she something?"

"She's something alright." I listened as I heard a line that was something about her unmentionables being so good, she screamed her own name during sex. "Sounds fantastic. What exactly are you hoping to achieve? Your regulars won't like this booming shit, they come here for a beer and a chat, and maybe to watch the game on your ancient TV. Perhaps you could have invested some money on updating that and getting decent cable service."

"Oh, you're such a downer, Frank. Get with the times. This'll draw in a new crowd, more money, some youngsters maybe. Pete's bar will be the new, oh I don't know, the new Chuck E. Cheese."

I looked at him. "You know that's a kid's restaurant with a giant mouse as a mascot, right?"

"Really? A mouse? Alright, maybe not Chuck E. Cheese then, but anyway you get my point. Something new. Speaking of, I've been practicing a new repartee, check this out." He cleared his throat. "A man and a giraffe walk into a bar."

"Jokes? That's your new repartee? Seriously?"

Pete ignored me. "They both get drunk, and the giraffe falls over in the bar. The man goes to leave, and the bartender goes, 'hey, you can't leave that lying there,' and the man says—"

"That's not a lion, that's a giraffe."

Pete slapped the bar and laughed. "You've heard it? It's great, isn't it?"

"Your new repartee consists of loud music and crappy jokes? I don't get it, Pete. I'd say don't give up your day job, but this is your day job." I placed the back of my hand on his forehead. "You don't have a fever, but I'm not sure what's come over you. I think you could take it down a notch or two—you know, just for starters."

Pete's smile faltered for the first time. "Too much you think?" He rubbed his face. "I dunno. Maybe you're right."

"Listen it's all good. Just not quite so loud and maybe some better jokes."

"Sure, sure," he said, turning the music back up a notch. "Beer?"

"Sure. And some earplugs. And no more jokes." We walked back to the bar, and I sat on the same seat.

As Pete handed me a beer, he said, "So how's Jessica?"

"She's doing okay. She had a mild concussion, and they kept her in for observation, but nothing was broken. She was lucky. A few feet closer and that explosion would have mushed her insides. Thankfully, the bulkhead where she was at shielded her from the brunt of it. I got scraped up some, though."

"Look alright to me."

I eyed him. "Thanks. A lot you know. Hell, maybe you're right. I was lucky too. The blast pushed me through the air a few feet, and I landed on my back, but it could've been worse.

"Anyway. It's over now. We got the fuckers. I took one of them down, and the enforcement guys found the other rat bastard trying to wire up another bomb. The MEs handed him over to the feds, and I hope they're waterboarding the fucker right now."

"So, what's the plan?"

"I'm gonna take a few more days off I think," I hesitated. "Something's off between Jess and me. I'm going to try and fix that too. We're s'posed to take *Serenity* out for a spin in the next day or two. Hopefully, we'll have a chance to talk then."

"Let me know how it goes," he said and went off to serve a customer that had just come in. I smirked to myself when the customer asked what was with all the noise.

I sat at the bar, sipping my beer, lost in thought. What was wrong with Jess? Or was it me?

Sixteen

This was supposed to be a winding down, put your feet up cruise aboard the *Serenity*. Beer was in the cooler, the fridge stocked. The day was gorgeous with a sky that seemed to stretch into forever, and at first, it was a good day.

We'd finally killed or captured the cocksuckers that had murdered Browning and Miner and prevented a major catastrophe. It wouldn't have just been a sunken boat in the channel, it would have blocked all shipping traffic from Corpus for months and polluted the entire ecosystem, perhaps irrevocably.

But thanks to the lead from King, and the help from the FBI, we'd nailed the bastards, so Carter and I were taking some R&R time aboard the *Serenity*. She still hadn't told me why she was acting weird, and we hadn't had a good chance to talk about that text she sent me when I was in Key West, telling me we needed to talk. Never a good thing in my experience. So, I thought a couple of beers, some sun and surf, the flap of sails and halyards dinging on the mast, and she'd relax enough to let me know what was going on in that beautiful head of hers. We cast off and cruised out through the shipping channel and into the Gulf of Mexico.

Chief of security aboard the *Nexus Joy* was Rory Jones, and he absolutely loved his job. As the sleek cruise ship slipped from its dock and got underway from Corpus

Christi, Jones slid to the ground from the top bunk of his girlfriend's cabin, a pretty blonde from Scandinavia. He pushed his legs into his white uniform pants, buttoned and tucked in his white uniform shirt replete with epaulets, and tightened his regulation white belt.

He couldn't get the belt to wrap around his girth quite as tightly as it used to, but for someone in his early fifties, and with a full head of mostly black hair, he thought he was doing all right. He was pretty sure he didn't look bad in a bathing suit either, and with plenty of beautiful women on board he was a happy camper. Women, who on shore wouldn't give him the time of day, certainly gave him more than that when at sea, and he wasn't complaining. He continued to dress, slipping on his white shoes sans socks, and slid out of her cabin on deck two midships in the bowels of the ship and went looking for his early morning coffee.

Jones considered sex just one perk of the job, and if he'd told his mates back in the UK that he had a Swedish girlfriend, he didn't think they'd believe him. Free food, free lodging, and carte blanche movement around the ship at any time of day or night were icing. As head of security, he always had a reason to be wherever he was, wherever that may be, whenever he felt like it. No one bothered him and his team of four. He reported directly to the staff captain, the second in command on the ship, and as long as nothing went wrong, he was happy as a pig in shit. And while he was in charge, he was damned well determined that nothing would go wrong. This was a cushy job, a perfect job for his rapidly approaching twilight years, and he aimed to hold on to it for as long as his dick still worked.

Rory's prior life had been as a British Royal Navy Chief Petty Officer. He'd sailed the seven seas, got the T-shirt that came with it, a small pension after dedicated service, several decorations from the First Gulf War, deployments all over.

It wasn't a bad life, he'd made many fast and firm friends, but it wasn't a life if you wanted a wife and two point four kids. It wasn't fair on a family being at sea for most of his career, so Rory had never married in the traditional sense, although he was married to the sea.

The *Nexus Joy* though? Man, he wished he'd known about this cruise ship gig sooner. It was a sweet deal. An acquaintance had contacted him shortly after he'd retired from the RN and asked him if he wanted to go back to sea. Rory was about to put the phone down when he heard cruise ship and immediately asked for more details, dreaming of sun, sand, surf and beautiful women. His job on the *Nexus Joy* couldn't have exceeded his expectations anymore even if he'd tried. And the *Nexus* was the best damn ship out there.

Jones pushed his way into the security office on deck five, near a bank of six elevators and the shore excursion desk, and nodded at his second in command, Georgie Reed.

"Coffee's fresh, just brewed it," Reed said, nodding to the pot, perched on a back shelf, as Jones came in. Strictly speaking, appliances weren't allowed outside of the galley, but Jones felt that as head of security, that rule didn't apply to his team, and they could go fuck themselves if they thought differently.

"Anything?" Jones asked, pointing his steaming mug at the impressive seventeen security screens, continually rotating through images of various parts of the ship. He thought seventeen was a bit too much for one man to stay reasonably focused on, but he didn't design the system and didn't really give a crap. Once they were underway, it was all smooth sailing. It was when they were docked that Jones knew it was possible for the shit to hit the fan. But it was as secure as he could make it. Each passenger had to have a shipboard ID, and it was scanned as they came on board. So far, the only trouble he'd had was a couple of idiots trying to smuggle drugs on board hidden in the hollowed-out heads of their golf clubs.

Jones took a sip of coffee and grimaced. "You sure this coffee is fresh, Georgie? It tastes like bollocks."

Reed turned to look at him, momentarily taking his eyes off the screens. "Well, if anyone knows what bollocks taste like, it'd be you, wouldn't it?" He shrugged. "I'll just have to take your word for it.

"Wanker. Any trouble?"

"Nada. Been quiet. Oh, except for a bit of trouble down on deck two. Seems like there was an officer down there in one of the crew cabins. Don't know what he was doing, but he was in there an awful long time."

Jones grinned, knowing Reed was talking about him, put down his coffee, and hitched his belt up a little, grotesquely emphasizing his bulge.

"I'll take that as a yes, or an I don't know," Reed said.

Jones was impressed. With such a large ship, it would have been easy to miss him slipping from one of the cabins. Reed was good like that. Jones couldn't do it, but Reed seemed to have a knack for looking at everything simultaneously. Which was why he usually had him on watch on embarkation day, when all the new hoi-polloi were coming on board. Reed could digitally sniff out trouble. It probably helped that they had state-of-the-art facial recognition programs running, and that background checks had been completed on all the passengers before they ever stepped foot on board. The *Nexus Joy* didn't take anything for granted.

Which was why it was a bit of a shame that Alpha and Charlie, the two Haqqani terrorists, slipped aboard so easily.

***

Once past the jetties and our course was set, I set the autopilot and sat down on the stern seats, across from Carter. She looked sad, and when our eyes touched, a ghost of a smile covered her face, there and gone so quickly it could have been a shadow.

"Frank, we need to talk."

I'd been dreading those words since the Key West text, and now they were out in the open. But this is what I wanted. To clear the air.

I coughed and swallowed to cover my anxiety and stood to check the horizon. Once I saw we were still clear of other traffic, I sat back down and said, "What about, Jess? I thought we...I thought everything was fine." I didn't.

"And that's one of the reasons we need to talk, Frank." She leaned over and touched my hand briefly, fleetingly. "I love you. I truly do. But we can't go on like this."

My heart fluttered. "Like what?"

She waved her hand around. "Like this. You and me. I'm broken, Frank. You deserve better than me, than this. You must have noticed how I've been. Jumpy, snappy, remote? I know you're not that oblivious."

I looked around to ensure nothing big was coming up behind us and then at the set of the sails. My voice cracked. "Jess, don't do this. Please. I love you." Carter was my all, my soulmate. This was ripping me inside out.

She looked away, but not before I saw her eyes were glossy.

"I know you love me, Frank. I just need some space." Her hands smoothed an imaginary crease on her shorts. "I can't stay here on this boat with you anymore. I keep having flashbacks to Black and what he did to me. I can't be the person you need me to be until I learn to deal with this properly. On my own terms."

I can fix this. "That's fine. You don't need to live on *Serenity*. Stay in your apartment, you're still paying rent, after all. I'll give you as much space as you need. It'll be like when we first met. We can take it slowly." I threw what I thought were all the right sentences out there. Grasping at straws.

She looked at me, tears now flowing freely down her tanned face. "No, Frank. It can't be like before. I'm not myself, nowhere near anything resembling my normal, and I don't want this to be my new normal. I can't pretend everything is okay, as it isn't, and this isn't fair to you. You deserve someone who can give you their all, and that's not me, not anymore.

"Black, what he did to me, I can't..." she took a deep, shuddering breath and held it in a moment before continuing, "I put him in a box in my head, but he keeps getting out." She wiped tears from her face. I wanted to reach out but couldn't move. "Even before I got hurt on board that tanker, I was having flashbacks, but getting hurt brought everything back with a punch. I was on that island again. With him. I can't keep doing this to myself.

"I've given it some serious thought, Frank." She'd been avoiding looking directly at me, but now she held my gaze. "I'm going to take a leave of absence. Tobias has already approved my temporary separation. It starts at the end of this month."

I stood up, checked the sails, scanned the horizon. Something was in my eye causing it to tear up, so I wiped it clear. "A leave of absence is two years, Jess. You didn't think to tell me this, didn't think to talk it through with me? I could have helped. We're partners, Jess, for Christ's sake. When were you going to tell me, or were you just going to disappear?" I didn't mean to sound bitter. I think I was in shock.

"You have every right to be angry, but it has nothing to do with you—"

"That's harsh, Jess."

"Don't make this about you, Frank."

"How can I not? We live together." I waved my arm around. "We share everything. Come on, Jess, please. Rethink this." I sat and grabbed her hand. "Let me in. We can do this together. Stronger together, remember?" I smiled at her, still holding her hand. That something was still in my eye, both eyes now in fact, as my vision was a little blurry.

She shook her head and pulled her hand back. I let her go. "This is my life, Frank, and I need to figure out how to make me be me again. I don't know if that's possible, I'm not even sure who me is anymore, but I do know it's not going to happen while I stay here, in Corpus." Her voice caught and hitched. She looked away and then back. "I do love you, Frank, truly. Maybe one day we can try again, but right now, with that bastard's shadow hanging over my every waking thought...I can't do it.

"Surely, you've noticed the night terrors, the distraction. I can't physically be as close to you as you want me to be. I just can't do it, and I hate myself for it a little more every day. I need to heal. And I can only do that by myself."

I was silent for a moment, looking out at the ocean. "Where're you going to go, Jess?"

She leaned back and followed my gaze to the horizon. "I don't know yet. Somewhere away from this heat." She looked across at the water. "Somewhere with mountains and streams, fresh air, no humidity. Somewhere that's not flat. I want to go off-grid for a while. I have some family in Tennessee, maybe I'll start there. I don't know yet."

I wanted to tell her it was still humid in Tennessee but didn't. I wanted to tell her I could fix it, but I couldn't. I sat back down, head spinning, gut churning, and said the hardest thing I've ever had to say to anyone, anywhere. "I understand."

In my gut, I knew this was it. She wasn't going to come back. I'm not sure if she knew at that moment herself, but she'd figure it out.

Carter looked even sadder, wiping the tears from her eyes and standing.

"Would it be too much to ask for a hug?" she asked.

It would. But I did it anyway. Her arms wrapped around me, her tears wet on my cheek, and I heard her whisper in my ear, "I'm sorry, Frank." I held on to her until she released me and then went below to dig that something out of my eyes.

It all happened so fast, as is the case with these things.

The pilot had finished his navigational duties aboard the *Nexus Joy* and was waiting for his ride back home. The large cargo hatch in the side of the ship was open, and he waited patiently for the pilot boat to come and pick him up.

The *Nexus Joy* maintained speed and direction as the coxswain on the pilot boat pulled alongside the open hatch. The coxswain executed the evolution flawlessly even though his current situation was a mite unusual in his experience, as he had a gun jammed to the side of his head.

It was usually a simple matter for the pilot to step through the hatch and down the small gangway, onto the pilot boat and speed away, back home. This time, however, the pilot hadn't even stepped foot onto the gangway before a silenced bullet slammed into his skull, spraying blood in an arc over the junior security officer standing behind him. Both men fell to the floor.

The security guard started screaming, gagging on the blood that was in his mouth, but another silenced round through his throat and one more for good measure through his forehead put that worry out of his mind forever.

I couldn't tell you if I was angry, sad or something in between. I knew I was numb, and I guessed I'd have to settle for that lack of feeling for the time being.

I was still below, and it was good that I didn't own a dog as I probably would have kicked it right about now. No, that's not true. I like dogs.

My cell phone was vibrating itself into a frenzy on the table, and I would have launched it over the fucking side, but the number caught my eye.

"Aidan, what's up?" I sat awkwardly on the couch, the weight of emotion making me feel heavier than I was. I caught a glance of Carter holding the wheel with a steady hand. She must have taken it off autopilot. I wasn't sure if I wanted to wring her neck or sob at her feet. I understand? I actually said, I understand. What the fuck.

"Agent Dalton? Are you there? I can't hear you," came Aidan's excited voice over the other end of the line. He was usually calm, so his agitation pulled me back into the conversation.

"Sorry. Yes, I'm here. What's going on?"

"The body cam. We've analyzed it and—"

"Hold up, Aidan. Start at the beginning. What body cam?"

I could almost feel him vibrating over the line with the urgency he needed to tell me something. He sounded exasperated.

"The body cam that was recovered off the dead security guard at Tower Two during the fire."

"Okay, now I remember. What about it?"

"Well, the heat damage was extensive, so we've only managed, just now, to analyze the footage. It was running the entire time Geller, the guard, was at Tower Two. He was stabbed to death, Agent Dalton."

"Okay." He was excited. I felt like I had to say something.

"No, you're not getting it. It was running the whole time. It even showed what happened after his death, up until the point of the fire. It fizzled out sometime after that."

I sat up a little, a little lighter. "What did you see, Aidan?"

"We saw who killed him, Agent Dalton. I didn't even need to enhance the video. It was clear as day. The guys on board the tanker? Neither one of them was the guy that killed Geller. That means at least one of them is still alive, still out there."

The spike of adrenalin temporarily flushed out the remaining heavy weight of emotion I'd been laboring with, clearing my head. For now, my personal problems would have to be put aside. I yelled through the hatch. "Jess. Put it back on autopilot and get down here right now."

Alpha climbed over the dead bodies of the pilot and security guard. Charlie soon joined him after he took care of the coxswain. The pilot boat, now without a driver, bounced alongside the *Nexus Joy* a few times, gradually losing speed and was soon lost from sight.

Alpha and Charlie unceremoniously dragged the two dead bodies by their feet to the hatch and shoved them over the side.

Once again, they were dressed in board shorts, with towels strategically covering their guns in one hand. In the other, they both carried nondescript backpacks. They headed for the bridge.

Seventeen

A modern bridge on a state-of-the-art cruise ship shouldn't have been as easy to compromise as it was. But, like everything else, complacency was the harbinger of doom.

Alpha and Charlie wanted to kill as many people aboard the ship as they could. The more casualties, the bigger the statement. They had no love nor hate for these passengers. It was what it was.

They did, however, have the makings of a plan. They couldn't randomly run around shooting people. That only ever worked in movies. They needed to control the bridge, engineering, radio room—which was attached to the bridge—and do it quickly. They knew security would be aboard and likely the only source of offensive weaponry. The passengers were screened too well for any of them to have weapons, even if they were in Texas.

The door to the bridge had a solid steel core, built to withstand any sea conditions, fires, and the occasional curiously determined passenger. But it wasn't designed to be impregnable. And why would it be? After all, the *Achille Lauro* was decades ago, and no one had been stupid enough to try to hijack a cruise ship since.

However robust the door was, though, it couldn't withstand detonation from a wedge of C-4 Alpha had just wired to the security keypad and hinge areas. C-4 has an explosive velocity of 26,550 feet per second, so Alpha doubted very much whether a simple bridge door, steel or not, could withstand such a force. C-4 was also malleable and safe until detonated with a separate detonator. You could shoot it or drop it, and it wouldn't explode, so Alpha was able to push a good portion into the doorframe around the keypad entry and hinges. He had plenty to spare. A standard C-4 brick is almost a foot long, two inches across and an inch and a half thick, so one block was more than enough, and just to be sure, Alpha used the whole thing.

They worked quickly, not knowing whether security or the bridge crew had noticed them yet. Charlie had pulled out a spray can from his backpack and sprayed black paint on the security camera lens above the door, just in case.

The two men ran about fifteen feet away from the bridge door, took cover in an adjoining passageway, and detonated the C-4. The result was hardly subtle. The explosion was deafening in the corridor. The detonation left a pungent chemical odor heavy in the air, and grey smoke filled the hallway. The amount of C-4 Alpha had used was definitely overkill as the whole bridge door was blown into the bridge and smacked the Philippine helmsman who was on duty, rendering him instantly dead.

The two terrorists ran back down the corridor to the bridge, through the still smoking remnants of the doorway, and threw a single M-84 stun grenade inside. Covering their ears, squeezing their eyes shut and turning away from the detonation, the effects were not as harmful as upon the bridge crew, who were still disoriented from the C-4 explosion. The optical and acoustic double whammy—sudden bright flash and near instantaneous deafening noise—was tremendous.

Walking calmly into the mess of the bridge, Alpha identified the captain lying amongst the rubble by the gold stripes on his uniform and shot him in the head. A crewmember cowering beside the radar got another shot to the head. The helmsman had already been crushed by the steel door.

In all, there were five other crew members on the bridge, and Alpha and Charlie shot them all, keeping only one alive, the most junior officer on the bridge, a single gold stripe identifying him.

"Name?" Alpha said. The stunned officer didn't say anything, so Alpha shoved his gun in the officer's gut, causing him to gag.

"Name? I won't ask you again."

"Maader. Rudolph Maader."

"Well, Rudy. You don't mind if I call you Rudy do—"

"What in the seven levels of hell is going on in here?"

An elderly man dressed in an off-white linen suit was making his way onto the bridge, flapping his hands at the smoke that was rapidly dissipating. Spotting Charlie but not really seeing him or how out of place he looked on the bridge, the old man started to wave an angry fist in his face. "I say, young man. I said what—"

Charlie shot him in between the eyes, turned to Alpha and shrugged. "I'll guard the door."

"Do that," Alpha said. "No, wait. Take care of the radio room. We're probably far enough from shore that cell phones won't work, so let's get rid of the only other way to call for help."

Charlie nodded and took down a fire ax clipped to the wall, hefting it in his hands.

Alpha smiled as he heard the smack and crunch of the fire ax. "Now, where were we?" He crouched down to Maader, where he had collapsed after being struck in the gut. Looking him in the eye, he continued. "My name is Alpha. I am now in charge. Understand, Rudy?"

Rudy looked around him and saw that there was no one left. He nodded. "Yes. Please don't hurt me."

"Rudy, Rudy, Rudy. Of course I'm not going to hurt you. We need you, Rudy. Now, tell me, what's your job on board the ship?"

"Third...third officer," he stammered.

"Excellent. Now, what are your duties on board? For instance, do you know how to drive the ship?"

Maader nodded again.

Alpha smiled and tapped him on the shoulder. "Charlie," Alpha called as he came out of the radio room. "Rudy here knows how to drive the ship."

Charlie grunted back, rivulets of sweat on his face, moving back to guard the open bridge door. "Maybe you could get him to fix the air conditioning while you're about it."

"Now, Rudy. We don't want to hurt anyone else, and I think that you deserve a promotion. How does captain sound? How d'you like that? I just saved you years and years of hard work, and you've only known me, what, less than a few minutes? You and me," he waved his gun between them, "we're destined for great things. All I need you to do is to follow my orders. Immediately and without question. Can you do that, Rudy?"

Maader nodded again, and Alpha patted him on the cheek, not quite a slap. "Good. Now just stay here while I consult with my colleague."

<hr>

"What the fuck was that?" Jones asked. It was a muffled noise from several decks away but still sounded out of place.

"Nothing. Maybe a wave," Reed said, turning back to his screens. He frowned.

"A wave couldn't have—"

"Hang about a second. What's that?" He pointed at one of the screens.

"It looks like the cargo area. Why's the hatch still open? Radio Mickey and see what he's up to, he should have been with the pilot."

"Security three, control."

When no one answered, Jones didn't skip a beat. "Get Roger down there."

After a couple of minutes, they saw Roger Mulford appear on the screen. Mulford was a walking skeleton with a paunch. Prematurely balding, bent of back, his white security shirt hung from his thin, weak shoulders. His hands shook ever so slightly, more when he hadn't had a recent nicotine fix, fingers stained an ugly yellow that matched his teeth. Rory and Georgie watched him on one of the monitors. It didn't take Mulford long to radio back.

"Boss. You need to come down here, right now." There was no broaching any argument, and Rory dashed out of the security office. Along the passageway and down three flights of stairs, through a 'Crew Only' doorway, and down one more passageway, his feet now slapping against the painted metal floor of the crew areas juxtaposed with the nice, carpeted passenger areas.

He saw Mulford and was about to ask what was wrong when he pointed a thin, reedy arm at the floor. Jones looked down. He knew what he was looking at as soon as he saw it.

"Fuck." He dashed to the open cargo hatch and stuck his head out, being careful to hold on to the side. Outside, he could see the sleek white hull of the ship slicing through the water, but nothing else. A few scratches on the hull, maybe.

He walked over to a phone secured to the wall in a small alcove and dialed the bridge. He would have dialed the emergency number, but that number was his. After seven rings, he hung up.

"Shit. Roger, the bridge isn't answering. Listen, I want you to go up there and see what's going on. Something's happened to Mickey and maybe the pilot, I don't know what. This blood though, whatever it is can't be good."

Mulford turned to leave, but Jones held his shoulder, turning him back.

"Oh, and Roger," Jones looked him in the eye. "Be careful, mate."

Mulford nodded and left.

"Jess, let's get *Serenity* turned about and head back in. Pull down the jib, we'll leave the mainsail up, and I'll crank up the motor, we'll make better speed."

I watched her whole body move in motion as she winched in the jib. Her butt was pointed at me, and my heart skipped a little. I swallowed it down. No more. She must have sensed me watching her as she turned back and gave me a fleeting smile. This was it then.

I pushed all that down, plotted the quickest course back to the T-Heads. We were a few miles out into the Gulf, and I didn't see anything on the horizon, save for the outbound *Nexus Joy*. I checked the radar, and we were far enough apart that our paths wouldn't cross.

Twenty minutes later, I thought I saw something and reached for my binoculars. "What's that?" I wasn't really talking to Carter, but she answered anyway.

"Give me the binos, I'll take a look. My eyes are better."

I handed them over, and after a moment she said, "It looks...like one of the pilot boats, but..."

"What?"

"It looks weird. It's not making way, just seems to be bobbing out there."

"See if you can hail them on the radio, see if they need help."

Carter went below to the radio, which was just beyond the hatch on the starboard side. She came back a minute later.

Shaking her head, she said, "No answer. Do you think they're in trouble?"

I sighed. "Fuck. I don't want to take the time." I also didn't want to leave them out here if they were in distress. "Fuck it. Let's find out." I turned the helm hard over to port, tacking, and put *Serenity* on an intercept course.

"Alpha, someone's coming," Charlie hissed.

"Be right there," he said to Charlie. "Rudy, now mate, I want you to take this ship south, toward Mexico, okay? No particular place, just out into the Gulf a bit and down a bit. Okay? And do it slow, no need to rile the passengers up."

Rudy nodded and gently picked himself up, looking nervously at Alpha, expecting a blow.

"Oh, and see what you can do to clean this place up, eh? Place looks shocking."

He walked over to where Charlie was near the door. "Now what have we got here?" They could see Mulford walking down the passageway, hugging the bulkhead, trying to be stealthy.

"This is just too easy, Charlie," Alpha said conversationally, ignoring Mulford's approach. "Maybe we should have done this all along, you know? Taken ourselves on a nice cruise, instead of that shithole commune in Afghanistan."

Alpha stepped out from his position beside the busted doorway, aimed his pistol at Mulford, and pumped three bullets into his paunch. Mulford slammed into the bulkhead and slid, for the first time in his life, almost gracefully to the deck, an ugly red smear covering the nouveau riche art on the bulkhead.

"Charlie. I need you to stay up here and guard the bridge. Make sure Rudy there keeps us on course. I'm going to make our presence felt most awesomely." He grinned, and Charlie laughed.

"Leave me with some fun, will you Alpha? Rudy doesn't look like he's got many jokes."

"Sure thing, I can do that." Whistling as he walked along the passageway, gun in hand, Alpha made his way to the more populated decks to cause hate and discontent, or as he would put it—necessary fun.

Carter and I motor-sailed to the pilot boat. When we got nearer, we let the mainsail down so we could maneuver a little easier. Up close, the pilot boat looked disabled, but what was weird was the lack of anyone on board. Even if something had prevented them from hailing for help on the radio, there should have been some sort of movement aboard.

As we got closer, I left Carter manning the wheel and went below for my replacement piece, another Glock. They still hadn't found mine yet. I checked it was loaded but refrained from ratcheting it like they do on TV. Really. It's always so stupid. It's the first thing you do when you load a magazine before you holster the weapon. Not every time you draw it. All these television and movie federal agents looked like idiots.

"Jess, come up on the lee of the pilot boat, nice and steady." Carter was a phenomenal boat driver, and she'd had plenty of practice with *Serenity* over the last few months.

I waited until we were within spitting distance, and gun at the ready, hailed them. "Ahoy on the pilot boat. Anybody aboard. This is the Coast Guard."

I glanced at Carter. She shrugged.

"Get me as close as you can," I said.

When we were a couple of feet away, I timed the rise and fall of the waves and stepped carefully across to the well deck of the pilot boat. I signaled Carter to back off and maintain a safe distance. I clambered below, letting my eyes adjust to the relative darkness, and stood silently for a moment.

It didn't look good.

I didn't recognize the man, but it was easy to spot he was dead as half his head was missing. A no-brainer. I know, I know. I can't help it. I searched the rest of the vessel, knowing no one else was aboard as it was a mostly open boat, with just a cramped solo bunk and small head.

I called Carter on my cell.

"Jess, where was the pilot boat going to or coming from? Can you find out? I'm going to see if the engines work."

"What did you find on board, anything?"

"Yeah. One dead guy. Looks like it might have been the coxswain. I'm going to wipe his brains off the console so I can see what I'm doing."

She hung up. I wasn't really going to wipe his brains off the console. It was smeared mostly on the starboard window, and I could leave that. I liked to think I was preserving evidence, but I really didn't want to touch something that should literally never see the light of day.

I checked the fuses and gauges, and it seemed all SAT and thumbed the starters for the two massive diesel engines. Within seconds, I could hear the roar of ignition settle down and a soft burble from the stern. Nothing wrong with the engines, then.

Carter called back. "Frank, the pilot boat was on its way to pick up the pilot from the *Nexus Joy*. They've been trying to contact the pilot for a while now, I guess we know why they couldn't."

"Jess, do you think this could have anything to do with our missing terrorists?" I said. The more I thought about it as the words came out of my mouth, the more likely it seemed. Here was a boat going out to pick up the pilot of the *Nexus Joy*. No pilot, dead coxswain. Maybe someone else hitched a ride.

I grabbed the radio. "*Nexus Joy, Nexus Joy,* this is the pilot boat channel one six, over."

I looked over at Carter, *Serenity* just off my port quarter. She could hear me on the radio and shook her head. I tried again. "*Nexus Joy, Nexus Joy,* channel one six, over."

I picked up the cell phone again. "Jess, it's these guys. It has to be. Call for backup, I'm going to get on board."

"Frank, don't be stupid. If it's the terrorists, they'll have a thousand hostages. Let me at least come with you. That ship is massive. You'll never clear it by yourself"

"No," I said, perhaps a little too harshly. Carter was capable and confident, but right now, I didn't want the distraction. She'd made herself perfectly clear where we stood, and the tiniest diversion, smallest little mind fuck could get me killed. I was also thinking of how she was hurt on board the tanker, and this was likely to be a one-way mission. I wasn't going to do anything suicidal, but I knew my chances weren't good and didn't want her to get hurt again. "Take *Serenity* back to port. Brief Smith, when you get some cell service, keep trying the radio as well. Get me some backup. I'm the nearest thing those passengers have got for help. Fuck knows what's happening."

***

Alpha was making his way down the passageway on the seventh deck toward amidships and the door to access the crew areas. Behind the façade of musicals, comedians, lush tropical plants, glass elevators, big band music, and nightclubs, inside bars, sky bars, outside bars, restaurants, and promenades there was always the working hum of seamless background crew activities. You didn't see the sous chefs or the waiters or the cleaners or any of the thousand crew unless they were in their allotted places. The crew had their own galley, berthing, entertainment, and back stairs, elevators, and corridors to get around. Heaven forbid a passenger should see a crew member off-duty or out of place.

The crew door Alpha was looking for wasn't hidden, it wasn't a big secret, it just wasn't advertised, and the average passenger never gave it a second thought.

Alpha soon found the door, discreetly marked as 'crew access only' and pushed the heavy watertight door open. Inside, the foot-dampening plush carpet from the passenger corridor was replaced in the crew corridor with a lovely shade of brown-beige linoleum.

Alpha was looking for the engine room. Having secured the bridge, radio room and two security guards, their chances of taking over the ship had significantly increased. He knew his chances of taking control of the whole ship were initially slim, but he and Charlie would do what they could until they got caught.

Jones dashed from the cargo loading area back to the security office. He needed to get back and unlock the gun safe.

He fumbled with the door code until Reed opened the door from the inside.

"What's going on, Rory?"

Jones took a moment to look at him. "Georgie, mate, I don't know." He ran his hands through his hair as he entered the office and slammed the door behind him, locking it. "There was blood. Down below. No sign of Mickey or the pilot or his boat. Just blood. No answer from the bridge, but we're still moving, so maybe that's just a glitch, although I doubt it." Jones paced in the cramped quarters as he spoke. "I sent Roger up there for a look see." Jones stopped pacing and looked at Reed, then the monitors, then back again to Reed, a thought percolating in his head. "Georgie, mate. You saw me come out of a cabin on deck two this morning." Jones nodded his head at the security monitors. "How come you didn't see anything going on where the pilot was? You didn't decide to take a shit right around then, did you?"

Reed's guilt flashed across his face, and he was about to answer when movement on one of the monitors caught Jones's eye. "Never mind that now, we'll sort it later," Reed said, pointing at a monitor. "Look, Roger's coming up to the bridge. He'll sort this shit out."

They both watched the security screens and were just in time to see Mulford hit the bulkhead, obviously dead, and a swimsuit-wearing man stroll nonchalantly past, a gun in his hand.

"Jesus fucking Christ. Georgie, keep an eye on that rat bastard while I open the gun safe. We're under attack."

I pushed the twin throttles of the pilot boat all the way, jamming them down the last bit to get every ounce of juice. The burly beast wallowed for a minute and then came up on a plane. I fumbled with the radar looking for the *Nexus Joy's* AIS signature. We'd passed it less than thirty minutes ago, so it couldn't have gotten too far, even if it was cruising at twenty knots. I set the radar at a mile, then five, then ten. At a range of just under ten miles, I saw a blip and the corresponding AIS identification.

"Gotcha." I set course, hoping I'd be in time to do something.

EIGHTEEN

I was able to make decent time getting to the *Nexus Joy* on the pilot boat, going almost twice their speed, and soon saw her white hull in the distance, then closer, then like a giant white whale plowing through the sea.

There wasn't any way I could sneak up on them. I could only hope that no one was waiting for me or watching. It was a risk I had to take. I hated going in blind.

Getting on board the *Nexus Joy* proved a little more difficult than I had imagined. I maneuvered alongside until the gaping yaw of the cargo hatch appeared like a huge mouth waiting to swallow me. The gangway was missing, and the hatch was up high. Knowing that this was going to take some skill and plenty of luck, I matched speed with the *Nexus Joy* and got within two feet of the ship. I had only a few seconds to make my move, as without the gangway I had to get up on the roof of the pilot boat to gain the height I needed to get aboard. There didn't seem to be an autopilot for the helm that I could see. There probably was, but I didn't have time to find it.

I steadied the helm as best I could. There was nothing with which to lash it into place, so I knew the wake from the ship would soon push the pilot boat away.

I kept my fingers on the wheel until the last second and then dashed out.

As soon as I let go of the wheel, the boat drifted. I scrambled up the ladder, onto the roof of the bridge, the gap between the vessels widening quickly as I went up. The gap became two feet and then three feet. I saw the blue of ocean water. If I missed getting on the ship, I'd likely be sucked into the screws of the *Nexus Joy*, which was less than desirable.

I backed up as far as I could go and launched myself from the edge of the pilot boat roof. Time seemed to slow down as if someone was watching my jump in super slow-mo. I landed ungracefully in a heap of legs and arms in the dimly lit cargo area and slid on something wet. Instinctively, I reached down and looked at my hand. It was red. Had to be blood. It didn't make me feel better that I was right about something terrible happening on the ship, but at least I knew it wasn't wasted effort.

I got up, drew my pistol, and headed to the stairs. I tried calling the bridge from a phone on the wall. No joy. I called Carter on my cell.

"Jess, I'm on board. I tried calling the bridge but there's no answer, and there's blood on the cargo area floor. No sign of anyone yet."

I heard her sharp intake of breath. "You were right."

I was, but it didn't make me feel any better. "Did you get ahold of anyone?"

She hesitated before replying. "I called Smith. He put out an alert to the Sector. The *Glorious* is being diverted from her patrol, but it'll be hours before she gets to you. Station Port A won't be much help either, their only offshore capable boat is in Charlie status, broke down late last night."

"Well, shit. Any good news?" I looked around, aware that I was exposed.

"Yes. The good news is that the air station is launching a helo and an HC-144. The helo is a Hitron helo in from the *Glorious* for routine maintenance, which they just finished. They should be in the air momentarily. You'll have sniper support from the helo in about twenty minutes."

I didn't know if twenty minutes was soon enough, but it'd have to do. "Alright. I can't wait for them to show up though, but maybe I can get whoever's on board out on deck. It might help. It might also panic the passengers to have a sniper helicopter aimed at them." I thought fast. "Call Smith, see if he can get me the schematics of the vessel and send it to my phone. Have someone keep trying to get through to the ship, there's got to be someone on board who knows what the hell's going on. I'm going to the bridge."

"What? Frank, you're breaking up. What did you say?"

"I said I'm going to the bridge. Carter? Carter, can you hear me? Shit." Must be out of cell range.

<hr>

Alpha had found the door to the engine room. It was secured with an electronic lock.

"Fuck," he said. He wasn't sure how to get past the security code. He didn't have any more C-4 to blow the door. He could only wait and hope someone went in or out. He looked at his watch and gave himself ten minutes. If no one had come by, by then, he'd have to think of something else. He slunk into a recess and waited.

<hr>

Jones, now suitably dressed in a bulletproof vest and equipped with a sidearm, hustled over to Reed.

"Where did that fucker go?"

"It looks like he accessed the crew door on deck seven. I lost him after that. We have something else, though." He pointed at the monitor where they could see someone in the cargo area on a cell phone. "This guy appeared out of nowhere. I don't know who he is."

"Shit. Do you think that's another one of these guys?"

Reed shrugged. "No way of knowing."

Jones thought for a minute. Three possible targets. One on the bridge, one in the cargo area and one in the crew area somewhere. Only two security guards left.

He snapped his fingers. "He's going to the engine room. The guy in the crew area. That's the only thing that makes sense. If they have the bridge, they need to secure the engine room. Otherwise, we can still control the ship. Radio the engine room. Tell them we have hostiles on board and to secure the place. No one goes in or out. See if you can call the Coast Guard before we get too far from shore. I'm going up to the bridge. Find the rest of the officers." He hesitated for a second. "I don't want to panic anyone, but the less people milling around the decks, the better, but we can't pipe that terrorists are on board. Shit."

Reed replied, "We could pipe something about a security drill. We need everyone to go back to their cabins as we have, I dunno, a gas leak?"

"No, we'd still have the stupid drunk bastards at the bars who don't give a fuck about drills." He slapped his head. "Got it. Pipe that there's been a severe outbreak of norovirus and we need to clean all the passenger areas, otherwise everyone will be sick. That should get people moving. The last thing they want to do on holiday is shit themselves. Tell them if we can get everyone back in their cabins for just one hour, we'll give them a hundred dollars, no, we'll give them free drinks for the rest of the cruise, if they can do it in the next ten minutes. That should have the arrogant little bastards scurrying back to their rooms."

Third assistant engineer Michael St. Louis had been on a real bender last night, tying one on in the crew bar. Every cruise ship ever built had a crew bar. A place where the crew could relax and unwind, out of the sight of passengers. Some crew bars were nothing more than a hatch that sold beer and was only open for a couple of hours every night, with white plastic garden furniture for seating. The *Nexus Joy*, however, treated the crew right. This crew bar rivaled anything on shore. There was a pool table, secured during rough weather, a couple of cork dart boards, comfortable leather couches and armchairs, a few large screen televisions, replete with Xbox and PlayStation consoles, and of course, a large, oak-paneled, full-service bar, open from 1700 to 0200. Every night.

St. Louis wasn't supposed to drink for twelve hours before his next watch, but he'd lost track of time. He'd been showing off for one of the pretty little Scandinavian cabin cleaners, trying to wow her with his prolific drinking abilities.

She was dressed in a tight, pale pink tank top, which did nothing to hide her impressive cleavage. Her almost-white blonde hair was tied in an elaborate braid that curled around from the back of her head to end brushing at the top of her cleavage.

"Listen, Mags. To become a Viking," he pronounced it Wiking, "You must do twenty-one shots of aquavit. You know of aquavit?"

She nodded.

"Is good," St. Louis was already a little drunk. "Aquavit make you strong. Made from potatoes." He pounded his chest in what he thought was an impersonation of a Viking.

She laughed. "And tastes like petrol. Are you a Viking, Mike? I thought you were from Minnesota?" Magdalena asked, leaning forward a little. She didn't care about becoming a Wiking, but St. Louis was cute in a handsome, boyish sort of way.

He grinned at her. "Tonight, we find out. Prost!"

He tapped his shot glass against hers and drained the glass. It was truly awful, and he held back his gag reflex as best he could, coughing slightly and turning away. Mags was Scandinavian and didn't even flinch as she drank hers, slamming the glass down on the table and picking up the next shot. She was already familiar with cruise ship Viking lore.

St. Louis knew the captain always did aquavit shots with the passengers on formal nights when all the passengers dressed up in fancy dresses and tuxedos, so he thought what was good for the goose was good for the gander, but what he didn't know was that the captain always substituted his aquavit for apple juice.

Although most crew on board were prolific drinkers, twenty-one shots of aquavit was only possible for the most hardcore of drinkers and borderline alcoholics.

St. Louis made it to twelve before he gave up. His speech slurred, coherent thought gone. How he made it back to his cabin, he had no clue, all thoughts of Magdalena gone from his head.

Now, the next morning, eyes bleary and bloodshot, he was staggering along the passageway toward the engine room, his shoulder sliding along the bulkhead for support. He'd brushed his teeth, gargled a ton of mouthwash, popped enough aspirin to cure ten heart attacks, drank a buttload of water, which he managed to keep down, and prayed he could get through his four-hour shift. By rights, he should have called in sick, but the chief engineer would have found out he was in the crew bar the night before, and well, that was never good.

He fumbled some foamies out of the bucket of hearing protection by the engine room door, dropping half a dozen in the process, shoving one in each ear. Carefully, he punched in the access code, the numbers blurring and swimming, having to redo the code twice before he got it right.

He never heard nor noticed Alpha come up silently behind him and slip through the door right after him.

I poked my head out of the crew door as near to the bridge as I could get and saw a shambling fat man with a gun in his right hand heading away from me.

I said in a loud, clear voice, "US Coast Guard. Drop the weapon."

The man stopped but didn't drop the weapon. He turned.

Nineteen

"Don't move. Drop the weapon," I said.

"If I drop the weapon, mate. It might go off. Don't want you to get jumpy now. Coast Guard you say? I'm Chief of Security aboard, Rory Jones is the name."

"Ease the weapon to the floor. Kick it away and turn and face me, hands over your head. Interlace your fingers."

"Supposing I did just that. Supposing you're not who you say you are. I've just given up my only defense."

"Good point, Rory, Chief of Security, but if I was a bad guy, I would have just shot you in the back of the head. I wouldn't be having this conversation."

"Fair enough."

He eased his gun to the floor and kicked it away, turning slowly. "You're that guy from the cargo area."

"Let's see some ID, Rory," I said.

"Now I don't really have any on me, save for my uniform under this bullet proof vest. What about you?"

Keeping a bead on him, I showed him my badge, which I'd hung from a chain around my neck. "Like I said, Coast Guard. We saw the pilot boat adrift, figured something was up. Come here, Rory."

He shuffled over to me, his eyes flickering between the gun and badge.

"Okay," Jones said. "I believe you're who you say you are. I'm going to slowly strip off my vest so that you can see my uniform. But we need to hurry this shit up. I've lost two men. There are at least two hostiles on board, I think one is on the bridge, and all this bullshit we're doing isn't helping."

"Better get that vest off quick then, Rory." I wasn't taking any chances. I didn't think this guy was a terrorist—a bit too long in the tooth and evidently English—but I didn't want to get shot either.

I watched him pull on the Velcro straps holding his vest on. His gut gave an almost audible sigh as the constriction left, and his stomach flopped out. He was wearing a white button-down shirt with the name of the ship stitched on over the left breast pocket and security stitched on the other side. I didn't think this overweight, middle-aged guy was who I was looking for.

"Okay, Rory. Put your vest back on. Who else is on your team?"

"Georgie. Georgie Reed. He's down in the office. Monitoring."

"Radio him."

He did. And then I could hear Reed ask Jones what he wanted over the radio speaker.

"Okay. I believe you, Rory. My name's Dalton, Frank Dalton. I'm a special agent with the Coast Guard. What's the situation?"

We shook hands, and Rory went to retrieve his pistol. Conferring in low tones, he said, "Like I said, I have two men down. Two left, Georgie and me. At least two hostiles. One is on the bridge, I think. The other is loose in the crew areas. If I were him, I'd try and get into the engine room, but I've put an alert out with the crew to stay put and not open the door. The passengers should all be in their staterooms, we told them there was an outbreak of norovirus."

I appraised Rory. He seemed to be holding up well, despite everything that was going on. "Good idea about the norovirus. What's the status of the captain and the rest of the bridge crew?"

"Unknown. The captain would have been on the bridge when all this went down, but I can't confirm that. Comms are down."

"There's a helicopter on the way, should be here in about fifteen minutes. They have a sniper on board. If we can flush out the bad guys, they can take a shot."

"Speaking of, who are these fucks?"

"We believe they're Haqqani trained terrorists. They killed two of my colleagues a few days ago. We think we disrupted their original plan and thought we'd caught them, but we caught a different cell, or the same cell working on a different target, not sure yet. We know these guys don't mess around."

"I noticed. I saw them kill Roger."

"Sorry about your man. Listen, it's your ship. What are the chances of us getting the bridge back?"

Rory shrugged. "I dunno, mate. I was on my way up there to see what was going on. There's only one way in and out, just down this passageway a bit, round the next bulkhead." He hesitated. "We'd be right in the line of fire."

The crew in the engine room didn't stand a chance. Alpha shot Third Assistant Engineer St. Louis in the back of the head as soon as he was through the door, stepping over his body and through to the Engine Control Room.

Inside the ECR, several engineers sat monitoring the electronic readouts, and Alpha shot them one by one.

The last alive, a great hulk of a man in grease-stained white coveralls, ran at Alpha with a giant wrench raised over his head, and Alpha shot him in the left knee, watching him fold, the wrench clanking harmlessly onto the deck.

Alpha walked over to him. "Now, mister?" he said, raising his eyebrows in question.

"Fuck you," the engineer spat out, writhing in agony on the floor, but glaring at Alpha.

"Interesting name, is that Chinese?" Alpha said. He stepped on the engineer's shattered knee. "Now, Mister Fuck You. I need you to tell me where the remote bridge control is."

"I said, fuck—" the engineer screamed in agony as Alpha pressed down on his shattered knee.

"Nope. Don't think that's it. It's straightforward. You tell me where the control is, and we can speed this whole thing up and get you some help, or I'll shoot your other kneecap, cripple you for life, find the control myself and leave you to bleed out. Which is it?" He increased pressure on the engineer's knee and aimed his pistol at the other.

"I don't have much patience, Mister Fuck You. One...Two..." Alpha pulled back the hammer of his weapon with his thumb.

"Okay. Okay. It's, aargh, it's on the panel over there."

"Show me." Alpha helped the engineer to his feet. "And don't be stupid." The engineer hobbled over to a bank of switches and levers along the bulkhead. He pointed at a lever that was labeled in two spots as Bridge and Engine Room.

Alpha turned the lever to Bridge, effectively giving the bridge full control over the engines.

"Now, that wasn't so hard, was it, Mister Fuck You?"

The engineer nodded, his face ashen, blood pooling on the deck from his knee.

"Why don't you go sit down and take a load off? That looks mighty painful."

The engineer nodded again and hobbled to the nearest chair. Before he got there, Alpha shot him in the head. "Not nice to be impolite, Mister Fuck You, and I don't think that was your real name. So, fuck you."

He looked at the engine monitors and saw a couple of engineers still in the main engine room, oblivious to what was going on in the soundproofed ECR.

Whistling idly, he left the ECR and went in search of the remaining engineers. Couldn't have anyone come in and change the controls back, could we now?

***

"So, what do you propose?" Reed said.

"I say we go to the bridge and blow these fuckers away," I said.

"I'm not sure, mate, but that isn't the soundest plan I've ever heard. Roger got blasted trying to do the same thing."

I looked at him. "All right. Your ship. What do you propose?"

"Your chopper that's coming. Snipers you said?"

I nodded.

"Might be that the sniper can take out the guy on the bridge. Those damn windows are pretty big. The sniper has thermal imaging?"

"That and more."

"Let's knock it on the head then. We should go find that other fucker. This one on the bridge ain't going nowhere."

"Georgie," Rory said into his radio, "you get a bead on that other rat bastard?"

"Just got a glimpse of him leaving the engine room area. Looks like he's heading for one of the top decks."

"Did the passengers go back to their rooms?"

"Most. There're a few stragglers. Mostly the ones already too drunk to give a damn."

"Fuck. Where's the biggest group of them?"

"Lido deck. Where the pool is, I'd guess about twenty, some are in the hot tub."

"Georgie. Keep looking for this guy, we're heading up there. Let me know if he pops out."

"Roger. Err, who's we? Did the staff captain get a hold of you?"

"The cavalry is here, Georgie. They sent General Fucking Custer to help us out. What's that about the staff captain?"

"He was on his way to the engine room to secure it. He wanted to arm the crew."

"No fucking way. And I hope you didn't let him have a weapon. I can't have a bunch of untrained waiters running around with pistols. Don't let anyone else in. Keep me posted."

"Fuck," he said. "That's the last thing I need."

"I thought you said the captain was on the bridge?"

"He is or was. Most likely dead. No, this is the staff captain."

I shrugged.

"You know, like the XO, second in command, not quite the head cheese—"

"I got it thanks. Lead the way."

<hr>

When Alpha left the engine room, disabling the code to the door so it wouldn't open for anyone else, he debated going to the bridge but decided to swing by the outside passenger areas. Maybe I'll find something worth my time, he thought.

Alpha never expected to get this far on board the *Nexus Joy*, the plan was fluid and ambitious, they didn't want to ransom the passengers, had no desire to bargain for flights to Libya or some other desert backwater, they just wanted to cause the maximum amount of fear mongering and damage they could manage before they died. The Haqqani probably had some game plan to capitalize on this incident, although Alpha didn't think this was what they'd quite planned on. But he was sure they would claim on network television that it was all Allah's will to rid the world of the unwashed American infidels or spin something similar. All Alpha wanted to do was remind America to wake up and protect itself.

Alpha climbed the wide carpeted staircase, banister tastefully inlaid with gold braid, until he got to the lido deck. He paused at the sliding glass door and could see the large swimming pool beyond. A few passengers were frolicking in the pool, laughing raucously at some joke.

The joke will be on them in less than a minute, he thought.

He ejected his magazine, checked his rounds. He'd reloaded after the engine room, and walked outside, pulling on a pair of almost entirely black Ray-Bans he'd had in a pocket of his board shorts.

"Hey guys," he said, waving his gun at the pool dwellers. "Can I join in the fun?"

Their laughing gradually fell silent, dull and muted as they saw the gun. The alcohol they'd consumed, large margaritas with cute little umbrellas, with an extra shot of Don Julio Anejo tequila—had numbed their brains and their reflexes, so they didn't move, just looked on mutely, not totally comprehending this man with a gun.

"Oh, come on, what happened to the jokes?" He crouched on one knee next to the pool and pointed his gun at one of the men. "Tell me a joke."

The man opened and closed his mouth, but nothing came out.

"Nothing?" Alpha sighed. "Okay. Not funny." Alpha shot him in the head.

Now the group started to move. The women screamed, the men shouted, surging to get out of the pool and away from this madman.

"Too late."

Alpha stood, and taking his time, shot each person in the head. He paused on the last person, watching him try to heave his drunken mass from the water, which was now tinged a dark crimson. His friends lying face up and face down, unmoving, tendrils of blood swirling in the water by the pumps and mixed by the thrashing of limbs.

"Hey."

The man continued to try and escape from the death pool.

"I said, hey motherfucker," Alpha said, walking around the pool until he was in front of the man. He pointed his gun at the man's face and waited a moment for him to notice.

The man froze when he realized Alpha was in front of him.

"Do you have a joke?" Alpha said. He looked at the man's vacant expression, bewildered and confused. Alpha sighed. "No, I don't suppose you do."

"No, no, no, no, no, no—"

Alpha shot him in the head. Headshots were Alpha's favorite. He never missed, not ever, and definitely not at almost point-blank range.

He walked past the pool, looking over the railing at the blue of the sea. He scanned the horizon, didn't see anything remarkable.

He whistled as he walked, a sonorous tune, long and without humor. A crazy glint in his eye. He walked along the deck, up some steps and toward one of the six hot tubs on board. This one was designated as an 'Adults Only' hot tub, although if it were full of kids, it wouldn't have bothered him.

You've just got to love a pistol with a suppressor, he thought. Not enough noise to alert anyone. These morons are still up here frolicking around, while I have control of the ship.

He walked right up to the edge of the hot tub and, elevated as it was, his pistol was hidden from view.

"Gentlemen," he said.

"'Bout time you showed up," a thirty-something blonde-haired Adonis said. He waved his arms at his friends. "Round of Coronas, make it snappy." He even snapped his fingers.

"Oh yes, sah, of course, sah, anything for you, sah," Alpha said, mock bowing.

The guy looked at him. "Hey," he said. "You can't talk to me like that."

Alpha laughed. "That's rich. Finally, somebody who's funny."

Alpha shot him first, then pumped the rest of his remaining magazine into the other three.

It was a waste of bullets, but he didn't care. He dropped the magazine and slammed a new one in, racking the slide.

"I just can't believe these assholes. Man, they just took all the fun out of this," he said. He shot the blonde again for good measure.

Alpha turned, intent on destroying the lives of more people, scanning the deck.

***

"Motherfucker, freeze," I shouted. Jones and I had come out onto the deck just a moment too late to save the people in the hot tub, but we could prevent him from killing anyone else. Jones had gone left, I'd gone right, and we were attempting to push him back toward the stern and corner him. There was nowhere to go except over the side, and the drop had to be easily over a hundred feet.

This wasn't the terrorist from the Haqqani Network I was expecting. Since they were an Afghan group, I was expecting someone, well, perhaps a bit swarthier. This guy...this guy was wearing board shorts and a tank top, for fuck's sake. The only thing that identified him as a shithead was the pistol trailing from his hand and pointing at me. He was a white dude, pale complexion, physically fit, defined arms, and short brown hair. Who are these guys?

The terrorist looked at me and loosed off a shot. I didn't bother hiding. From that distance and with a silenced pistol, I knew the round would go wide. Silencers are good for close work.

He turned, ducked down, ran to the rail, and looked over the side. I knew the jump would be too much. It was a straight drop.

He ran a few feet further and saw Jones approaching from his other side. We had him.

"Put the weapon down, fucker. We've got you surrounded. There's no way out."

He glanced over the side again and edged a few feet toward Jones. "You have no clue what I'm capable of, and I don't like your tone. My name is Alpha. Who are you, anyway."

The guy had a weird way of talking, some sort of New England WASP accent. I did my best Mark Wahlberg impersonation out of *The Departed*. It felt right. "Who am I? I'm the guy that does his job. You must be the other guy." I took the time to edge closer. "I'm also the guy that's going to stop you." If the instructor of the negotiation class I took could see me now.

I took a chance and dashed across the deck toward him, keeping a low profile, gun raised. Jones had his flank covered.

Alpha waved at us and then incredulously backflipped over the railing of the ship. I ran to where he'd jumped and looked over the side. I was dumbfounded. Nothing. All I could see was the rolling surf, no splashes. It was a straight drop. I looked at Jones. He was looking over the side too.

What the fuck? "Anything?" I asked.

"No. Crazy fucker how could he possibly have—"

And then we heard screaming, suddenly cut off, from the deck below.

TWENTY

"Here give me a hand," I said. Jones grabbed my belt as I hitched myself over the railing so that I could look down. One deck below us, I could see the cabin balconies. The slider directly below us was open, the curtains billowing slightly in the wind. "Pull me up."

Red-faced from being upside down, I said, "One deck below, I think he made it to the balcony."

Jones looked at me as if I were mad. "There's no way he could have back flipped off of here, dropped straight down and landed on the balcony. It's just not possible."

"You heard the screams. It's possible, it's only about ten feet max. They call it Parkour. It's French, some sort of acrobatics shit. I don't know. Maybe he had some escape planned, maybe he had a rope. It's ballsy for sure. All I know is he was up here and now he's not. Now, how do we get below?"

"Follow me."

We ran back, the swimming pool tinged red as a dawn sunrise. I didn't falter. I knew we had to get this guy, needed to stop him from creating any more slaughterhouses.

Down two short flights of hushed carpeted stairs, along another carpeted hallway.

"Which room?" I asked.

"It's got to be one of these three. I'll use the security override. Be ready."

I nodded. Jones got his card out, kept on the end of a retractable wire hooked to his belt. He swiped the card through the lock and pushed the door open wide with his left hand. I came in low, gun up. The cabin was larger than I expected. A small corridor opened to a larger room with a queen-size bed, full desk, and a floor to ceiling sliding glass door. The room was empty. The slider was closed.

"Not this room."

Jones nodded. We exited and went to the next room.

Same procedure. Jones ran the key card, pushed the door open. I came in low. I knew instantly this was the right room. The slider was open, the curtains were floating with the breeze, and there was a red stain against the wall. Beneath it, crumpled in a heap, was a semi-naked lady, mid-forties. She looked like she would have been a fun person.

We checked the rest of the room. Closets were empty, the oversized head was clean. Nothing.

"Fuck. Georgie," Jones said into his radio. "You get anything from deck ten, starboard side forward?"

Reed's scratchy voice came out of the speaker. "Nothing in the last few minutes. Let me scan around."

We walked back to the stairs, guns at our sides. "Who is this guy again?" Jones said.

"He's a terrorist. We know he came into Corpus a few days back. Two of our guys on a routine patrol along the beach spotted them, got in a gunfight. Our guys took out two of them but lost their lives. We're pretty certain there were only four in that cell."

"Sorry about your guys. I know how that feels." Jones cleared his throat. "There's more than one cell, then?"

"Not entirely sure at this point. We do know that in apparent retaliation, they took out the federal building downtown and then tried to sink a fully loaded tanker in the port."

"Seriously?"

"Yeah. We caught the two on the tanker before they could do any major damage to the ship, although they killed a lot of the crew. We thought we had them all. Obviously," I waved my hand around at the ship, "we didn't find them all. Looks like there was more than one cell."

We paused at the corner of a corridor and peaked around the bulkhead. There was nobody there, so we continued to move, scanning constantly. I continued in a low voice. "When they took out the federal building, they killed a security guard, his body cam was still running, recorded the whole thing, but it was damaged in the fire. I was out sailing this morning when they recovered the images on it, compared it to the fucks on the tanker, and realized we hadn't got them all.

"I was on the way back to port when I saw the pilot boat adrift." I shrugged. "The rest you know."

Jones's radio crackled. "Hey, boss. I don't know where he's been, but it looks like that guy is heading to the bridge now."

We looked at each other. "Let's try and head him off," Jones said. "I know this ship better than he does."

I followed his lead, down passageways, through crew areas, cutting across gleaming marble floors and past glass-walled elevators in the passenger areas. Jones motioned to me to keep quiet, and I guessed we were close.

He leaned in toward my ear and said in low tones, "Just round the next corner."

"Hey guys," Reed's too-loud voice crackled over the radio.

"Shit," Jones said, scrabbling to turn the speaker down. I looked around in alarm, and we ducked back a few feet, in case Alpha had heard. Alpha. Stupid fucking name.

"Shit, Georgie," he took a breath. "What's going on?"

"Good news, boss man. The Coast Guard called. Their helicopter is about three mikes away."

"Mikes?"

"That's what they said."

"It means minutes," I said.

Jones glared at me. "I know what it means, agent."

I put my hands up in supplication. "Just trying to help."

Jones visibly relaxed, breathing deeply, momentarily closing his eyes. "Sorry. Bit tense. Do you know what the chopper pilots are going to do?"

"At a guess, they'll take up a position where they can get a shot off, but far enough that they won't get shot themselves. Beyond that," I spread my hands wide in a half shrug. "I don't know, not an airedale."

"Georgie, get back on the horn, tell them we have at least one bad guy on the bridge. See if they can do anything about that. If they can tell us how many total are on the bridge, that'd help too."

"Roger."

I caught movement at the end of the passageway and lightly punched Jones's arm to get his attention. He looked at me, then down the corridor.

"Let's go," I whispered.

Crouching and running again, we covered both sides of the passageway. At the turn, a junction split into a thwartwise passageway, and I caught a flash of board shorts slipping around the bulkhead. I didn't want the guy to have any avenue of escape. I thought we'd cornered him before. I was wrong. I would not be wrong again.

"He must have seen us," Jones said to my shoulder, just behind me. "He's trying to get around us and get to the bridge. We have to stop him."

I wanted to say, no shit, but refrained. It wouldn't have helped right now. Instead, we picked up speed, Jones taking the passageway across from me. We'd cut him off.

I ran full tilt to the corner, sliding to a static-worthy stop on the carpet and poked my head out. I saw board shorts. His back was toward me.

I poked my head and shoulders out from the bulkhead, just like I'd been trained many years ago, using the bulkhead as a makeshift barricade. Alpha was just standing still, not doing anything. He had something in his hands, hidden from my view.

I took a bead on him. I couldn't miss. "Freeze, motherfucker," I shouted.

Alpha jumped, fumbling with whatever was in his hands, almost dropping it and trying to catch it. I squeezed the trigger a millimeter. I couldn't let him get a grip on his gun.

"Drop it."

I saw Jones's head poke out from the other end of the passageway. I could see the whites of his eyes open in surprise. He stepped out, right into my line of sight.

"Frank, don't shoot."

Alpha dropped to the ground, crouching to pick up his gun, Jones making him jump again and losing control.

"Rory, move, you idiot."

"Frank, it's not him. It's not Alpha. It's just a kid."

I eased off the trigger, pointing the gun in the air, and the boy turned. A kid of about seventeen, in board shorts and a tank top, wandering the hallways.

"Fuck. Kid, I nearly shot you. Why aren't you in your cabin?"

"Huh?" he said, pulling out a bud from his ears, the sound of the bass suddenly and instantly identifiable from his earbuds. In his hand was his phone. He was fumbling with his phone when I saw him. It was a phone he'd almost dropped. I'd nearly killed him.

Sweat broke out all over my body. I holstered my weapon and ran my hands down my shirt, trying to wipe them clean. I leaned on the bulkhead, legs shaky. Fuck, that was close.

I looked at Jones at the other end of the corridor and mouthed my thanks. He smiled, and I smiled back, relieved at the close call, but then his smile froze in place as his brain exploded, skull, gray matter, and more blood than seemed possible, sprayed and splattered against the opposite bulkhead. Jones slowly collapsed to the deck.

I stood up and ran towards the kid, who was still standing, gawking. "Down," I screamed, rugby tackling him so that he fell quickly. I felt a puff of air skim over my head. Just in time. I crawled over the kid so that I was in front of him, motioning for him to stay down, and crawled toward Jones.

As I got closer to him and closer to the corner, I saw another bullet hit Jones's midsection, barely jolting him, like the solid whack of a spoon onto solid Jell-O. Hitting the bulletproof vest, unnecessary.

When I looked up, the passageway was clear. I slammed the butt of my gun down on the floor. I looked for Jones's radio, but it had broken in the fall. I was on my own again.

I ran back to the boy. "Where's your room?"

"Just, just, down there," he said, pointing.

I went with him. Made sure he was safe. "Lock the door. Don't leave, don't open it. Keep your slider locked. Stay put."

He nodded.

I left him and ran toward to the bridge.

I slowed as I got nearer, moving silently. I could see the body of who must have been Mulford. He looked like he'd been dead a thousand years already. His head looked shrunken, mummified, chest caved in. There was also another body of an old man.

I stepped over both, my eye on the shattered bridge door in front of me. I couldn't really see what was going on in there. I glanced behind me. I didn't know if Alpha had snuck in, or if he was off somewhere else, shooting some other poor innocents.

I kept low and against the port bulkhead to give me a wider field of view of the inside. I was about ten feet away from the door.

Then five.

Then three.

I stopped and listened at the threshold. I still couldn't see anything.

Then I heard a faint whup whup whup of rotors and the distinctive bree sound the French motors made on the MH-65 Dolphin helicopter. I'd recognize that sound anywhere. Help was here.

I stayed low, as I imagined the sniper on the helo taking a bead on whoever was inside. I didn't want them to take a shot at me, as they didn't miss. Ever.

I heard a sound like something substantial hitting something wet. The whup whup whup and bree sounds from outside suddenly became more noticeable, and I knew they'd taken the shot.

I waited a moment in case they were going to shoot again and heard nothing. I stood up slowly and poked my head inside the bridge.

If I thought the swimming pool had looked like an abattoir, then this was the abattoir's big brother. The place reeked of feces, blood streaked the control systems, and bodies were piled up and dumped unceremoniously along the port side near the bridge wing. What a fucking disaster.

There was one guy left standing. He was wearing the ship's uniform—white shirt, black slacks—blonde hair sticking out from a white sailor's cap.

"Hey," I said. "Over here, by the door. I'm Special Agent Dalton. What's your name?"

He stared at me, his eyes haunted, cast in semi-shadow by the visor of his hat. I glanced behind to make sure Alpha wasn't creeping up on me.

"Rudy."

"Hey, Rudy. Is there anyone else up here with you?"

He shook his head. "Okay, Rudy I'm coming in."

I holstered my weapon and held up my badge in one hand. I knew the sniper would be able to see me through the expansive bridge windows; he'd be able to see my badge. Hopefully, someone had told him I was aboard.

After a moment I saw the helo waggle from side to side and move off a ways. They'd seen me. I turned back to Rudy.

"How many of them?" I asked, casting my eyes around, looking for threats.

Rudy just stared at me blankly.

"Rudy, how many bad guys were on board?"

"They are legion." He pointed to the floor and kicked a body next to him. "This one was called Charlie. The other is Alpha."

They are legion? "Is?" I said. I'd only heard one shot from the sniper. "Rudy, is Alpha up here, on the bridge?" The hairs on the back of my neck sprang out, and I drew my weapon, scanning the room, not looking at Rudy, seeing through him. That was my mistake. That and I was too close.

Rudy suddenly pivoted at the waist and lashed out with his leg. I stumbled back, but not far enough before he connected with my knee. Pain lanced through it as my leg buckled and I fell, my hands out. My eyes opened wide in horror as I fell. I couldn't avoid the soul next to me, and my hands and arms sank deep into his shot-out chest cavity.

I pulled my hands free. A sucking, slurping sound came with them, and I rolled, just barely dodging the kick to my ribs. I should have fucking known. Rudy was Alpha. He must have gotten here before me and the helo. If there ever was a Rudy, I didn't know, but Alpha had changed out of his board shorts and into the ship's uniform. Replete with hat.

I'd dropped my gun when I'd sunk cock deep into that guy's stomach and dove for it now. I didn't radio my intentions, but Alpha guessed and aimed another kick, this time at my head.

I rolled onto my back, going from a forward dive to a back skid. Parkour be damned, this was Frankour.

The blood helped. I tried not to think about it, sliding on someone else's guts.

Like in the movies, I slid up to my gun, grabbed it, and shot at Alpha. Or rather I slid past my gun, missed it and came up short against the captain's chair.

Alpha clambered over the bridge controls and made a dash for the starboard side bridge wing. Anybody else would be stuck out there, perched high above the ocean. Based on what I'd seen this shithead do before though, I knew that small space wouldn't hold him.

I scrambled up, shoes slipping on some intestines. My entire body was covered in blood, and my clothes clung to me like I'd been caught in a blood thunderstorm.

I shot at him, but he was already gone. I glanced out the bridge window, and the helo, its fuselage a shimmering fiery red in the sun and heat, must have seen unusual movement because they came in closer. I hoped they had a bead on

Alpha. I wish I had a radio so I could call them. I held out my badge again so they didn't shoot the freak show I must look like.

I looked over the edge of the bridge wing and saw him running toward the stern. I shot but missed. He didn't stop running. There was no way my Frankour was good enough to get me over the bridge wing, the deck was at least eighteen feet down, and inboard from where I was.

I ignored the pain in my knee, shambled back out the bridge door, and attempted a half jump over Roger, whose desiccated skull grinned at me, seeming to say, you're fucked, Dalton. I didn't disagree with him.

Down the passageway, three flights of stairs and out the doors. I was on the Lido deck again. The helo was hovering sideways, the sniper visible, about two hundred feet in front of me, more toward the stern than I was.

I limp-sprinted along the deck, arms pumping, legs striding. My knee groaned and screamed with each thump of shoe on deck where Alpha had kicked it. I grimaced and ignored it, the adrenaline that was surging through my system trying to take care of it for me. They'd be hell to pay for it later. If there was a later for me.

As I got nearer the helo, it started to go up. So I did too, taking the stairs two at a time, a little whimper of pain escaping from my lips.

Now the helo was about amidships. I couldn't hear a damn thing over the whup whup whup and bree noise its engines made. I looked at the sniper. I could see him clearly as he was only thirty feet away, and lifted my arms and shrugged, hoping he understood I didn't know where Alpha was.

He mimed making a phone call with his fingers. I swiped my hand, palm down, fingers extended and flat across my neck and shook my head.

First Parkour and now mime. The French would be proud.

I didn't know where Alpha was but didn't see how he could escape from a sniper. His best bet would be to stay inside. Hide in a cabin and assume someone's identity. There was no way he was getting off this ship. By now, the *Glorious* would be en route, along with a small fleet of other Coast Guard assets.

I glanced up and saw a figure way high, climbing the outside of the twin smokestacks. The stacks themselves were a good sixty feet tall, each ten feet wide, perched on a platform another twenty feet in the air. A lot of it was for show, rather than any engineering necessity, great big billboards emblazoned with the *Nexus Joy* logo.

It had to be Alpha that was climbing the stacks, but what the fuck was he going to do up there? He was making himself an easy target.

I waved at the helo, pointed at the stacks and hobbled over to the ladder. It was time to prove Frankour was a match for Parkour.

I had to holster my weapon so I could climb the ladder. It was a seriously long way up. At the end of the ladder, it went through a gap in an overhanging platform, in between the two stacks. The helo wouldn't be able to get a good vantage point if he holed up inside. I couldn't imagine, even with his acrobatics, how he could escape from up here. Why do bad guys always seem to go up when they're cornered? Must be in the genes or something.

I stuck my head through the gap and quickly pulled it back, trying for what they call a sneak peek. The peripheral images can be processed by the brain after you get out of the way, the idea being that you keep your head.

I kept mine but felt the puff of air and heard the ricochet. The afterimage I had was of him on another ladder, about halfway up, in between the stacks. For a second, I thought maybe he was trying to get inside the stack and back inside the vessel, but that wouldn't work. Maybe Alpha didn't know that, and I could trap him.

I glanced out again and took a shot in the area I thought he was. The bullet ricocheted off the metal of the stack but did little else.

Another quick peek, I couldn't see him. Taking a chance, I ran up the last few steps and rolled on the platform closer to the stack to provide some cover. My knee screamed at me, so I screamed back at it.

I crawled forward, eyes scouring upward. Still no sign of him. I edged ahead some more until I could see the ladder where I had spotted him.

There, at the top. I saw him fumbling with something above his head. I wasn't sure what it was, but I had a clear shot. I steadied my breath, waited for the dead space in between my heartbeats and fired.

The shot seemed to take forever to hit its mark. I was a good forty or fifty yards from his position, but prone and with the time to aim...

My bullet fell short of center mass. The wind in between the stacks must have thrown it off, but I clipped his right calf.

Alpha faltered for a moment on the top rung of the ladder, only just regaining his footing.

I fired again, aiming to the left and higher to account for the drop in velocity and the wind.

I couldn't tell exactly what he was doing at this distance, but he was fumbling with something he'd hooked over a wire. The wire, festooned with lights, was rigged from the top of the stacks to the bow. At night, the lights were turned on, making the ship look like a giant Christmas tree.

As I pressed the trigger, Alpha jumped. I stood, tracked, aimed, fired again, and ran to the ladder. My shot missed.

It was this thick wire he'd jumped for, hooking something over it and holding onto the ends, like a makeshift zipline.

It didn't look like the wire would hold him. It was sagging, meant only to secure lights and small triangular flags, but he was still sliding away. If I didn't stop him, he might be able to get far enough and low enough along that he could drop to the deck.

I turned back to the ladder, momentarily out of view of Alpha, and heard the concussion of a high-powered rifle shot.

Sliding down the ladder, feet either side, hands gripping tightly, I ignored my knee again. Deal with it Dalton.

I ran around the stacks and saw Alpha hanging from his wrists, his hands caught in his makeshift zip line strap. He wasn't moving.

The helo was hovering alongside the ship. My view from the stacks had obscured them. The sniper had taken the shot. For a trained sniper this must have been as easy as a fairground duck shoot.

I waved at them and turned back to find the fire ax I'd spotted secured to a bulkhead.

Fire ax in hand, I went awkwardly back up the ladder to where the wire was secured, hefted the ax, and swung.

My first hit just bounced off, but the second one dug in enough that the wire parted, and I heard a dull thud as Alpha fell to the ground.

Wearily, adrenaline purging from my system in concert with the pulsing pain from my knee, I climbed down the ladder for the last time.

I limped over to Alpha, looked at him motionless for a moment, and kicked him in the head. I wanted to make sure the fuckwad was really dead. He didn't move.

I limped over to a bulkhead that was in the shade and slid carefully to the ground.

EPILOGUE

It was a few days after the events on the *Nexus Joy*. The ship was back in New Orleans, the FBI, ATF, CGIS New Orleans and a bunch of other letters were on board completing witness interviews, crime scene analysis and whatever else they were doing. As I was part of the incident I was debriefed but wasn't invited for the actual investigation. I didn't care. I'd done my part.

There hadn't been any other attacks and strangely the Haqqani hadn't claimed either attack. Counterintelligence gurus were looking at that. Way above my pay grade. We were still on high alert, but felt safe, for now.

In all, there were thirty-seven dead passengers and crew on the *Nexus Joy*. The doctor on board, a swarthy, bearded man of Asian descent and few words had collected the deceased and made room for them in the makeshift morgue as best he could for the trip to New Orleans.

Ships like the *Nexus Joy* expect to lose a few elderly passengers on every cruise, but they couldn't possibly be prepared for the extent of this savagery. A reefer that usually housed Grade 'A' beef was commandeered for the purpose. I guess we're all just meat in the end.

The pool was drained and cleaned. Alpha's bullets hadn't done much more than cosmetic damage to the décor.

The staff captain was rousted from his hiding hole, and he took control of what was left of the bridge.

When I left, the engineers were still trying to break into the engine room. Not having any handy C-4, it might take them a while, but they did have oxyacetylene torches, so you never know.

The Coast Guard helo with the sniper had to return to base, and I wasn't about to wait until we got to New Orleans to get off, so once the radios were in working order, I hailed a cab. So to speak.

Or at least I took priority for a ride back home. I left the details up to Smith. In the meantime, I'd found a quiet area and eased myself to the deck. My knee was throbbing more now the adrenaline was wearing off and it hurt to walk. Hopefully I hadn't ballsed it up too much.

Luckily for me, the *Nexus Joy* had a private helo landing pad, pretty swish for a cruise ship, but vital I guess for the clientele they had on board. Whatever. These rich folks'll have something else to talk about now when they get home besides what ports they visited and what Doris was wearing to dinner. I took the elevator up to the flight deck and sheltered from the rotor wash behind a door.

With the flub-flub-flub of spinning blades and the whir of the turbine, navigation lights flashing, a person in an orange jumpsuit waved red and green batons around and guided the helo down to the deck safely. I exited the door I was sheltering behind and ducked down so as not to have my head accidentally sliced off as I ran to the helo's open door. Once on board, I buckled in and pulled a set of headphones on so that I could talk to the pilot. I was the only passenger.

The pilot encouraged me to sit back and relax, and I did just that, watching out the window as we hovered and slowly went straight up. The cruise ship looked kind of dainty when we were a few hundred feet up. The water was a crisp blue azure, lightly awash with whitecaps, visible even from up here. We turned, and I lost sight of the ship as we headed back home. I rested my head back against the bulkhead and closed my eyes. I was tired. The emotional roller coaster of dead CGIS agents, my colleagues, my pals. Terrorists running around and finding Lewis like that. I thought he was long gone in the wind. I guess karma really is a bitch.

Perhaps the most significant emotional blow for me though was losing Jess. I knew she needed her space. She was a changed lady after Black. I didn't know what to do. We'd tried our best, given it our best shot, but it wasn't meant to be. I sighed. Maybe it was time for me to think about retiring, get out of the Guard. I'd have to give that one some thought.

On the *Nexus Joy* the passengers were told an element of the truth—that there had been a gunman on board, but he'd been dealt with by security and the US Coast Guard. The passengers, of course, had cell phone footage of the helo from their balconies, and with so many passengers missing, family and friends bereaving, the story would break soon.

Anyway, that was all a few days ago. Now, I was muscled up to the bar at Pete's, my leg stretched out on the stool next to me and my knee in a brace. Turns out Alpha had done a real number on it, and it was going to take a few weeks to get back to working level, at least that's what the doc had said. I'm not sure I could sit still that long. Luckily, nothing was torn, just a bad strain, so there's that at least.

Pete was hosting a going away of sorts for Carter. I'd come to terms with her leaving, and although I wasn't happy about it, I knew it was the best for her.

"Beer?" Pete asked.

"I thought you'd never ask," I said.

Behind the bar, Pete reached into a reefer and pulled out a frosty one, popped the top and placed it on the bar in front of me.

I took a swig, savoring the coolness and said, "What happened to that fancy speaker system you had installed?" I nodded at the wall where a compact wall mounted jukebox now sat in its place.

Pete smiled a little sheepishly. "You know, you were right. I—"

"I'm sorry, could you say that a bit louder for those in the back? I was right?" I couldn't hide the smile.

"Come on. Yes, you were right. I had a few complaints and well, realized it wasn't really me or the bar. I got the jukebox so people could choose what they want. And besides, I make a few bucks from it." He shrugged. "Seems to make people happy."

I heard the door open and turned toward it. Smith came in, walked over to me and we shook hands. "Don't get up," he said. I ignored him.

"Beer?" Pete asked.

"Sure, thanks," Smith said, and then to me, "how's that leg?"

"Oh, you know, boss. Should be good to go in a couple of weeks, maybe sooner."

Smith looked at me. "That's not what I heard from the doc. Said you'd be out for a lot longer than that."

I shrugged. "Ah. What do they know?"

I was saved from further inquisition by the bar door opening again. Carter and Hutchins walked in and over to the bar. Pete set them up with drinks.

It was odd seeing Carter and knowing we weren't together anymore. I wasn't sure if it would ever get easier. Carter had moved her stuff off *Serenity* and while I appreciated the extra space, *Serenity* felt empty without all her gear. I think she knew something was up.

"How's the leg?" Carter said.

"Everyone with the leg. It's fine, Jess. Thanks for asking. Be back to work next week."

Smith raised his eyebrows at my statement but didn't say anything. Carter smiled but it didn't reach her eyes. "Sure."

I was saved from awkward small talk by Doctor Hutchins. "Hey doc," I said.

Frank," she said. She reached down and hugged me. "I wanted to say thank you, for everything you did." She looked at Carter and Smith. "For everything you all did. This was a tough one."

"A toast," Smith said, raising his glass. "To Browning and Miner, may they rest in peace."

We clinked glasses and drank and then poured a slug out onto the floor. "For Browning and Miner. Gone but never forgotten." Pete didn't mind. He knew the tradition and joined in.

After a moment of silence and after glancing at me, Pete said, "So Jess, where is it you're going?"

"Tennessee, I think. I have some distant family out that way, and they offered to put me up until I find a job."

"You know," Smith said, "that your temporary separation is for two years and it's supposed to be subject to worldwide assignment when you come back. But if you want, I'll put in a good word so you can come back here."

Carter looked at Smith then glanced at me. I knew what she was going to say before she said it and I was right. "Thanks, Tobias. Honestly, I don't know what I want right now, but I'll certainly consider it when the time comes."

I knew she wasn't going to ask Smith. I don't think she was coming back to the Coast Guard. Or here. Or to me.

Carter and Hutchins drifted down the bar to talk to Pete. I watched them for a minute. Damn, I was going to miss her. I looked away before I got that thing in my eye again.

"Frank," Smith began. "I want you to take some time off...Time to heal."

"That'd be great, Tobias, but I've used a lot of leave this year already. I have a few days of light duty left, but I'll be back into work probably around the end of next week. And honestly, I don't think I really want to be by myself right now. Too many memories, you know?"

He nodded and took a long pull of his beer, signaling Pete for another one. He looked at me and raised his eyebrows. I nodded. He held up two fingers to Pete.

"I may have a solution," he said. "Have you heard of an island called St. Croix? It's in the US Virgin Islands."

I nodded. "I've heard of it."

"Good. They have a Resident Inspection Office out there. It's a small Coast Guard detachment, with about five people, and the lieutenant has requested some CGIS support, ostensibly to round up some illegal passenger charters."

I groaned. That was the last thing I wanted to do.

Smith must have seen the look on my face. "Hear me out. I said ostensibly. I need a reason for you to be there, but really what I want you to do is rest. Come by the office next week when your convalescent leave ends. I'll have orders for you to fly out there, help the lieutenant and then rest, for...How long do you think it will take to clear up the illegal charters, Frank?"

I thought about it. Realistically, about two, three days tops, and then a day or two for paperwork. "Hmmm. I dunno. Could be tough. Six weeks?"

Smith choked on his beer. "Don't take advantage, Frank. Tell you what, I'll cut your orders for thirty days. If you haven't sorted the problem by then, we can reassess. But when you come back, I want you in fighting condition. And listen, try not to get into any trouble while you're there, okay?" He looked at me. "I mean it. Stay out of trouble."

"Sure thing, boss." We clinked beers.

This was a nice surprise. The boss man hooking me up. Rum, sandy beaches, tropical water, monkeys on scooters, did I say rum? What could possibly go wrong?

THE END

"Fair Winds and Following Seas"

AFTERWORD

D ear Reader,

I can't thank you enough for joining me on this journey, and for taking a chance on me and Frank and picking up a copy of Deadly Tides. Your support is incredibly meaningful to me, and I truly hope the story has left you on the edge of your seat.

If you found yourself wrapped up in the twists and turns of the plot, and loved the book, I would be immensely grateful if you could share your experience in a review. Every word you share makes a difference to an indie author.

Stay connected for more thrills! Follow my journey on social media: facebook.com/shippwrites and Instagram.com/shippwrites for behind the scenes glimpses and updates.

FREE BOOK: To get exclusive content and be the first to hear about my new projects, please join my book club at Shippwrites.com and enjoy a free short story, Death & Dollars, set between the first and second books and unavailable anywhere else.

Thank you again from the bottom of my heart. Your support is the lifeblood of an indie author, and I can't wait to share more of Frank's adventures with you. You can join Frank in his next adventure Lethal Shores.

Jonathan.

ABOUT THE AUTHOR

Jonathan, a Chief Warrant Officer in the U.S. Coast Guard on the cusp of retirement, finds his true north in the world of storytelling. His desk, a microcosm of his dual life, is both a tactical command center and a cradle for his literary creations. Here, amidst the hum of duty and the clatter of keys, his faithful dog stands guard, ever alert for snack intruders.

His writing blends the thrill of maritime pursuits with the nuances of everyday life, capturing both action and introspection with equal flair. His tales are windows into worlds where duty collides with the narrative, and the high seas meet high stakes in prose. Rich in authenticity and peppered with humor, Jonathan's stories offer a glimpse into that world.

His readers laud his ability to turn everyday experiences into gripping narratives, while his critics find themselves disarmed by his unwavering gaze. Jonathan writes not just to fill the impending quiet of retirement but to continue the legacy of a life lived at full sail. His stories are more than just words; they are a testament to a journey filled with both waves and words, and it brings not an end but a new chapter in his odyssey of storytelling.

When not writing, Jonathan enjoys long walks, short naps, or is that short walks and long naps? and the occasional moment of existential panic about whether he's using semi-colons correctly.

Thank you for following him on this journey.

ALSO BY

Dangerous Currents

Deadly Tides

Lethal Shores

Acknowledgements

If you came with me on this journey, I'd like to thank you, dear reader, for making this journey possible. Without your support I wouldn't be able to continue to write, and you wouldn't be able to read anymore of Frank's adventures.

So again, thank you.

You can always reach me at <u>Jonathan@Shippwrites.com</u>